THE FALL AND RISE OF DAZZLE QUILL: ARTIST

HOWARD G AWBERY

1

Today was yesterday's tedium, repeated. Tomorrow will be more of today. The day after that will be much the same. Six days in a row, no change. Thank the Lord for Sunday for it will break the sameness of the weeks, which appeared to be creeping into months. If Sunday could be described in words, it would be poetry, the days of the week would be prose. If Sunday had a smell, it would be that wonderful chocolate aroma when a bar is unwrapped for the first time and expectation of the first bite is high. If the days of the week had a smell it would be boiled cabbage – a smell that percolates through the corridors and classrooms of every school, every day. All adults who had ever been to a British school can bring the smell to mind in an instant.

The rhyme and verse of Sunday was a wonderful change for the town's artist society. That is, as long as it wasn't raining, and if it was, the day would revert back to another tedious, boiled cabbage weekday. For when it was raining, nobody ventured along the beach promenade at St. Cuthbert's Bay on the south coast of England. The only people on the promenade on wet days were folk with dogs. Dogs who did not want to be out either, whose demeanour said it all. However, if the day promised sunshine, then the anticipation of the local artists would be high, and they would hurry to secure a good pitch to display their work on the promenade.

Life had barely changed for thirty-seven-year-old Dazzle Quill in the past nine years as an artist. Now in the spring of '94 he had little to look forward to, was resolutely single, and lived in a two-up, two-down cramped terraced house in St. Cuthbert's Bay. A crumbling, Victorian, sea-side town once famous for its ozone and easy proximity from London. Now it was populated only by newlyweds and the nearly dead, and, of course, some optimistic artists.

Unfortunately, the artists' main problem was St. Cuthbert's Bay Town Council. The misguided, but well-meaning town council had generously granted permission for local artists to ply their trade on Sundays along the promenade wall. Great news for the artists. However, what they had not taken into account was that the holiday accommodation owners had asked another department to co-ordinate a meeting of all interested parties, and it had been agreed that Sunday would become the changeover day for holidaymakers, in order to reduce traffic congestion. Therefore, the artists' potential customers were either coming or going, arriving late or leaving early.

The fraternity of artists joked, 'Once there were only two lies in life – "Of course I'll love you in the morning!" and "The cheque is definitely in the post." Now there is a third lie – "We are from St. Cuthbert's Bay Town Council and here to help you!"'

Life was tough enough for the local artists without the town council's cross-eyed thinking.

Dazzle sighed deep into his morning mug of tea as he remembered the rain dribbling down the polythene hanging on a make-shift frame, barely protecting his paintings the previous wet Sunday. Despite his best efforts with his tent, watercolours did not fare well in the damp conditions. Holidaymakers caught out on such a wet afternoon would hardly glance at his display of paintings through the inadequate, translucent covers as they hurried past. Those who did stop would shelter while shaking the rain off their umbrellas inside his camp, complain about the dreadful weather, and then brave the elements once again – without making a purchase. Occasionally, dogs cocked their legs inside his tent as a protest against their enforced walk in the rain.

If enthusiasm for the future had a colour and came in a tube of watercolour paint to be mixed on Dazzle's palette, the tube would be squashed flat, with every last drop used up.

In a reflective mood, Dazzle acknowledged he had felt the same way after leaving teaching. Fresh faced out of teacher training college at twenty-two, he had begun working at the local secondary school teaching art. Or, more accurately, refereeing local fishermen and farmers' youngsters. He desperately tried to enthuse into them the wonderful world of art as he knew it. All his energy went into exciting the students in forty-minute bursts, which appeared to be about fifteen minutes longer than the maximum time either he or they could tolerate.

Exploring the wonders of Turner, Lowry, Constable or even early Banksy received only cursory, disinterested glances from them. Due to fishing or farming being the only employment in the area, his pupils preferred to bury themselves in the pages of *Farmers Weekly*, which contained

3

the latest fat stock prices, or the much glossier *Marine Diesel Engine* monthly magazine.

His determination to inspire the youth of the day slowly bled out of him due to school management politics, minute-by-minute lesson planning that stifled any hint of creativity or spontaneity, and the senseless charade of inspection preparations. It was all beyond his comprehension, and when the nonsense inveigled into his evenings and weekends, he knew it was time to call it a day.

After six long, exhausting years, Dazzle's ambition had well and truly expired. He vowed never to step inside a school again, and so didn't.

Dazzle turned his thoughts to the day ahead. Nearly a vegetarian through financial necessity, he survived by preparing a huge vegetable casserole every Sunday, which lasted him until Thursday. Bargain bags of bruised vegetables were sold off cheaply at the end of Saturday trading at the fruit and veg market in St. Cuthbert's Bay town centre, and sometimes he got lucky with a propensity of parsnips, onions, carrots, celeriac and potatoes.

Occasionally he was not so lucky, ending up with a bag of radishes, cabbage and Khloe rabbi. How he hated Khloe rabbi. It all depended on who served him.

If it was the knowing manager of the vegetable stall, he and Dazzle always had the same conversation:

"How's your goat this week?"

"My goat is well, thank you for asking," Dazzle would reply.

"Remind me of his name."

"My goat is still a she and her name is Doris."

With that, the manager would throw into Dazzle's bargain bag of bruised veg a few large carrots and a couple of good eating apples saying, 'Tell Doris, these are from me.' And he would wink at Dazzle, saving his embarrassment and continuing the pretence.

Dazzle was always profuse with his thanks, on behalf of Doris.

To make ends meet, Dazzle reluctantly rented out his second bedroom to a forty-six-year-old unemployed cartographer named Iorwerth ap Jenkins, pronounced 'Yorworth' and further shortened to 'Yorrie'. There had never been a huge demand for cartographers in the town of St. Cuthbert's Bay, or anywhere else for that matter, and a supposed persistent bad back prohibited this particular cartographer from accepting alternative employment.

Yorrie had moved into St. Cuthbert's Bay town only a year or so ago from way up in the Welsh Valleys – an unpronounceable, long Welsh village name from where his family hailed.

At first, Yorrie presented a vapid personality to Dazzle, and the world alike, but like all Welshmen far from home, he became staunchly Welsh and ready to fight anyone who denigrated Wales or the Welsh.

How Yorrie survived was a mystery to Dazzle, for his tenant lived on cornflakes, fish and chips, Chinese takeaways, beer and roll-ups. Yorrie's stick insect physique reflected his poor diet and lack of exercise (Dazzle had seen more fat on a chip!), and he was regularly puffed out climbing the thirteen narrow stairs in the tiny house. What Yorrie did all day was also a mystery to Dazzle as he seemed to have no friends and never spoke about how he spent his time.

By necessity, they shared the lounge area of the house in the evenings and occasionally recounted the day's events to each other. Last night, their lively banter went something like this:

"Do anything spectacular today, Yorrie?"

"Well, not really spectacular, Daz, but I did finish last week's Sudoku. The junior one that is. Beyond me is the adult one. And you?"

"Well, I went shopping in the town and got a really good bargain. They were selling twelve toilet rolls for the price of ten."

"Wow. Could I have the two free ones, please? Or perhaps you could reduce my rent by the same saving, isn't it?"

"Dream on," said Dazzle, without looking up from his free local paper.

They occasionally confronted higher levels of life's quandaries, such as: Should the toilet paper come off the front of the roll or should it come off the back? Other evenings, generally after a couple of beers, they debated problems like 'the train problem': A runaway train will kill five people but if you redirect the runaway train, it will only kill one person. The problem being whether to intervene or not. Or 'the puzzle of Theseus's ship: If all the parts of a ship are replaced over time, is it still the same ship?

Neither Dazzle nor Yorrie was really stimulated by these conversations, especially when one disputant had to think in his first language then translate arguments into English.

Dazzle Quill's existence had reached a new nadir. However, his life had not always been so downcast. His secondary education had been significantly influenced by a young art teacher by the name of Miss Cartwright. It was Miss Cartwright who encouraged him to take up art seriously. However, if she had taught blacksmithing, Dazzle would have ended up working the bellows in a forge, shoeing shire horses and making garden gates, such was her attraction. At that time, when he was nearly seventeen and she was about twenty-four, he was secretly infatuated by Miss Cartwright and all her encouragement. He hung on her every word.

As Miss Cartwright tried to teach art to the rest of the class, Dazzle would be in a world of his own, mesmerised by the light on her hair as she walked across the room. When she was close to the window, it was corn coloured and had sheen and bounce. Further away from the window, it appeared much darker but glossier. He struggled to take his eyes off her and memorised her image. As soon as he was home, out came his watercolours as he tried to capture the still fresh imagery.

Miss Cartwright was a passable artist herself and inspired Dazzle far more than any of the other kids in his class, whose post-school employment aspirations peaked at working three shifts in a factory chicken farm or cleaning the barnacles from the hulls of fishing boats in dry dock. She encouraged him to enter painting competitions on behalf of the school and magazine competitions privately. Even he was surprised by his successes.

Now at thirty-seven, and to stave off the inevitable first part-time job followed by the second part-time job, leaving little time to paint, he occasionally undertook small commissions from lonely locals wanting him to paint a picture of their house to send to their children who were mainly living abroad or Stoke-on-Trent or Milton Keynes. A gentle reminder that their 'parent' was still alive.

Dazzle also ate frugally and hardly ever drank wine (only if it was on offer on the bottom shelf at the supermarket). He worked every day in his inadequate studio which doubled up as the shared lounge. Seldom did he enjoy the result of his toil. His best work generated about £150 on a dry, sunny day when folk were in a good mood. On a wet, miserable weather day the same picture would only generate about half that. At the moment, he was just managing.

As more artists fell by the wayside, Dazzle Quill did not need a crystal ball to see a future working for the council collecting rubbish on the beach beckoning. But what else was he to do?

2

The days rumbled on. Nothing changed, nothing happened.

Yorrie continued to do whatever Yorrie did. Dazzle continued to paint his landscapes of St. Cuthbert's Bay, mounting his easel on the back of his front door. Every day he complained to himself about the poor light and every day it made no difference.

Occasionally, Yorrie would come home unexpectedly, swinging open the front door and bouncing into the lounge only to receive a swath of cloud colour across his face. A row would ensue. Yorrie would shout that if Dazzle locked the bloody door, it would never happen, and Dazzle would shout that if Yorrie whistled or knocked before entering it would be avoided. Their spat wouldn't last long but conflict would occur again if there was a choice of rugby or football on the TV that night.

It was after one of these spats that Dazzle noticed Yorrie hadn't been out for days. By Wednesday, the dustbin wasn't full of fish and chip paper or Chinese takeaway boxes, as usual. The bottle bin was still empty and Dazzle couldn't smell the pungent stench of roll-ups lingering upstairs. He also noticed that weight had dropped off his flimsy Welsh tenant – weight he could ill afford to lose. He asked what was wrong.

"Hungry I am. Not been out for food for days," whimpered Yorrie. "My stomach thinks my throat's been cut."

"One of your dad's sayings?" inquired Dazzle, looking up from his free paper.

"No, my nan's when her afternoon tea was a few seconds late."

"Why are you so hungry? You on a diet?"

"I'm on a no-money diet," said Yorrie flatly.

"How?" asked Dazzle, folding his paper.

"Well, you see, it's like this. It's all the fault of Grace Chapel, the pop singer."

Dazzle was mystified. "How on earth can Grace Chapel be the reason you're hungry?" he asked.

"Well, I listens to Grace on my transistor radio up in my bedroom while I'm reading the racing pages. She inspires me to choose wisely before I puts a bet on."

"I'm not following you. How does she inspire you?" queried Dazzle.

"Right, I'll explain. She sings a song like *Hi Ho Silver Lining* and I look for connections to the song in the names of the runners in the paper. I put my whole GIRO on a horse named Goldilocks last week. Silver and gold, see."

Dazzle, eyes wide at the tenuous connection, asked the obvious question, "And did it win?"

"No, still running it is."

Dazzle shook his head in disbelief. "When was the last time you ate anything?"

"Monday."

"There's still some of my vegetable casserole in the kitchen. Help yourself."

"Wow, thanks Daz, you're a lege."

"Anything else I should know about?" asked Dazzle as an afterthought.

Yorrie hesitated before answering.

"Well, yes, the DSS have stopped paying me 'cos I won't takes a job."

"Why won't you take on another job – still because of your back?"

"That's right. It's as fragile as glass, as I told you. If I do manual labour, I'll be laid up here for weeks. And a cartographer I am, not a bloody hod carrier on a building site. I can't stand heights neither."

Dazzle sighed. "Go and get some food down you and we'll talk later."

Yorrie could not get to the kitchen fast enough. At the door he stopped and turned towards Dazzle. "My old Dad used to say, 'Do a good deed in this world and it will be another diamond in your crown in the next.'"

Twenty minutes later, a much happier Yorrie returned to the lounge and settled down. He belched noisily.

"Sorry."

"Right, here's the deal," started Dazzle, launching into his prepared speech. It is time for things to change. "On Mondays, you clean upstairs."

Yorrie yawned loudly. Once he had processed the suggestion, he sat up abruptly.

"What, even the bathroom and the bog?" he asked, astonished.

"Especially the bathroom and the bog because of the state you leave them. On Tuesdays, you clean downstairs." Dazzle folded his arms.

"What, even the kitchen and scullery?"

Dazzle nodded. "And on Wednesdays, you sort out the back garden."

Clearly taken aback, Yorrie threw his hands in the air. "What, mowing and stuff? Whats about my bad back? You hadn't thought of that had you? The hedges are nine foot tall. Have you any idea how far the garden goes back? Have you ever ventured all the way? I'd need bread crumbs or a ball of string to gets back! There are probably wild campers squatting at the bottom."

"And fairies, probably," continued Dazzle without hesitating. "On Thursdays, you sort out the front garden and paint the front of the house."

"Ah, now, that's not so bad," agreed Yorrie, no doubt relieved the front garden was the size of a postage stamp, and the front of the house was equally small.

"All this in lieu of rent for three months," ended Dazzle.

"Can I lie down for the rest of the week?" Yorrie asked.

"No. On Fridays, you're free to do odd jobs for other people like car washing or bar work and what money you make, you keep. Same on Saturdays. On Sundays, you work with me on the promenade selling my pictures."

Dazzle unfolded his arms as Yorrie contemplated his offer. "Well, what do you think? Fair trade?"

"What about food?" asked Yorrie.

"That's what Friday and Saturday are for. You earn as much as you can, and you can cook for both of us a couple of times a week."

"Mmm. What if it's raining on Wednesdays when I'm supposed to be gardening?"

"Wear a mac."

"What if it's raining cats and dogs?"

"Wear a sou'wester and a mac!"

"Aha, what if it's cold and raining? You haven't thought of that, have you, Daz?"

"Wear a vest, a sou'wester and a mac!"

"OK," said Yorrie resignedly.

"Oh, I nearly forgot," remembered Dazzle, "no more fags in the house. That means nowhere, not even hanging out of your bedroom window."

"OK." Yorrie shrugged.

"That's settled then," said Dazzle as he walked to the kitchen, pleased to have asserted himself.

Moments later, he came back to the lounge. He was cross. "And when I said help yourself to some of my vegetable casserole, I didn't mean for you to eat three portions in one go!"

"Sorry," said Yorrie, sheepishly. "Good it was too."

Dazzle swallowed his annoyance but warned, "Any lapses and you are out with all your worldly goods – two carrier bags and a duffle bag – just as you arrived. OK, Yorrie?"

"OK," he agreed.

3

Yorrie doing the cleaning and tedious housework during the week (such an anathema to any artist), freed Dazzle to paint more and expand his stock for sale on Sundays.

It meant Dazzle could take half of his art down to the promenade and leave Yorrie to watch over it while he went back for the rest of the display. To be fair to him, Yorrie did his share of carrying and setting up.

However, one Sunday morning, as the predicted weather was so promising, they decided on an unusually early start to secure the best pitch.

Changing their pedestrian start to Sundays three weeks into their arrangement, Dazzle left Yorrie on the promenade with half the stock while he went back to get the rest.

As Dazzle pulled the second half of the stock in a small handcart towards the promenade, Yorrie was excitedly waving at him to hurry up.

"What? What's so exciting? You're acting like a puppy with two willies," quipped Dazzle as he got nearer.

"You'll never guess what just happened! Not in a million years. Not in a million, million years. I've just made my first sale for you, Daz. My very first. I'm over the moon!"

"What! What did you sell?" asked Dazzle, surprised.

"A lady wanted one of your paintings and couldn't wait till you got back, so I sold her it."

"Which painting?"

"You know the scape of the bay in the evening light that we both like? Full price I got for it too. £150 cash!" said Yorrie, waving the notes at Dazzle."

"Well! Really well done, Yorrie. I'll make an art dealer out of you yet," replied Dazzle, genuinely pleased for his tenant, and himself.

Excited beyond words, Yorrie continued basking in his success story. "What do you reckon about that then, eh? Full price! Do I get a commission?"

Dazzle should have known there would be more to it. "As I said, really well done," he replied, glossing over the request and turning back to the handcart. "Now help me set up the rest of the pictures so we can sell them all."

Yorrie hesitated and Dazzle tensed, waiting for a second plea. He breathed a sigh of relief when Yorrie appeared to think better of it and started helping to unload the little cart.

A few minutes later, however, he added an afterthought.

"Mind you, I had to do a BOGOF to clinch the sale."

"What?" Dazzle straightened rigid. "A buy one, get one free? Why, which other one did she want?"

"That one you said you were only 'quite' happy with. The one you've just finished."

"Yorrie, that one had a £195 ticket on it!" Dazzle groaned. "How long ago was this? Which way did she go?"

"Towards the town." Yorrie cocked his head in the general direction.

"Oh no! She could be anywhere by now." He groaned again, shaking his head, before hurrying off along the empty promenade and shouting back, "And don't do any more f***ing BOGOFS!" Dazzle sped up. It was a long promenade and would take an age to reach the town, even now he was jogging.

The first stall he passed was the candy floss stall. Despite his current mission, Dazzle couldn't help but think of the dentist's scourge when he smelled that childhood treat. How a spoonful of something in every mother's kitchen cupboard could be transformed into pink cotton heaven by seaside alchemy was beyond him. Many times, he had watched an ordinary man inexplicably spin simple sugar into pink cotton! Magic.

It was nothing short of a miracle, thought Dazzle as he hurried past. Although it was now sold in polythene bags rather than on traditional sticks due to bloody health and safety nonsense, Dazzle knew not a single child who had ever been impaled by a candy floss stick!

The stall holder waved, his expression curious, probably as to why Dazzle wasn't stopping to chat, as he normally did.

Whenever one is in a hurry the delays mount up, and so they did for Dazzle. The next interruption was a long line of beach donkeys crossing the promenade. He had to wait patiently for they were all tethered nose to tail, so he couldn't slip between them. He never knew there were so many donkeys on the beach, and he never knew they walked so slowly from the lorry then down the slipway. Didn't they all know he was in a hurry?

Neither did he know that as soon as they started to walk, they would all (yes, each and every donkey, without exception) do their ablutions on the pavement. First Dobin then Red Rum, Desert Orchid and Trigger followed on, then Shergar... And on, and on. The smell was appalling. And they all looked sad. Why were they sad? It was Sunday and not raining. As soon as the last quadruped passed, Dazzle leapt over Becher's Brook of donkey poo and urine and resumed his quest, hand over his nose.

His thoughts turned back to Yorrie. He wondered why anyone would consider doing a BOGOF with his paintings. They were good enough on their own without incentives. Dazzle was cross. He still had some distance to cover, so broke from jogging into a trot.

Next, he passed the rock stall displaying every colour of bull's eye, lolly pop and stick of rock imaginable. Despite his potentially expensive quest, Dazzle couldn't help but smile when he thought of the time the stallholder had to sack an employee for always turning up late to work. The stallholder told the latecomer he could work till Friday, pick up his wages, and then move on. It was a very bad move as upon examining his stock of rock the following week, the stallholder found he had nearly a mile of neatly cellophane-wrapped sticks of red rock with 'Bollocks' written right through them. He blew a gasket!

Shortly after the rock stall, a panting Dazzle turned into the busy High Street that led into the town. Slowing to a walk due to necessity and exhaustion, he immediately scanned the area, his gaze alighting on multiple people and locations, but he was unable to spot anyone carrying his paintings. At that moment, he nearly gave up hope as he was gasping so much he would be unable to hold a conversation with anyone even if he did catch up with them.

Disconsolate, he wound his way past all the cafés and shop fronts and was just about to head back to the promenade empty handed when he saw two painting-shaped packages, wrapped in brown paper and string, leaning against an empty table outside a café.

Inside, he joined the only customer at the counter, she had shoulder length dark hair and wore a floral blue, summer dress. The woman turned, smiled at him and carried her coffee and croissant out to the table with the two packages. Dazzle noted she had a slim figure that would turn heads in a crowd as she replaced her purse inside her Moroccan leather shoulder bag.

Dazzle ordered a coffee to go, paid, and followed her outside.

"Hello," he said nervously, his breathing slightly less ragged now.

"Hello?" she replied politely.

"Do you mind if I ask if your packages are paintings?' He dipped his head towards them.

"They are." She smiled.

"And did you buy them on the promenade?"

"I did. Why do you ask?"

"Well, the person who sold them to you works for me and had no right to let you have the second painting for free. I know you have no obligation to, but please could I have it back?"

The woman smiled again but her eyes were obscured by great big sunglasses that he had an urge to remove. "Yes, but it will cost you dinner tonight!" she said.

This took him by surprise. He was speechless. Dazzle looked at the woman and noticed she had manicured, natural-coloured nails. She wore sandals and her toes were also manicured and natural. She took off her sunglasses and there wasn't a scrap of makeup on her face, but her skin was lightly tanned. Wow, she is pretty, thought Dazzle. He knew he had to speak soon but he was struck dumb.

She held out her hand as she introduced herself. "I'm Mandy, by the way."

Dazzle placed his own coffee on the table, shook her hand and pulled up a chair beside her. Now more composed, he smiled.

"Hi, 'Mandy, by the way'. I'm Dazzle Quill."

Anticipating the next question, he continued, "Before you ask me how I ended up with a name like that, well, I'll tell you. When my proud father first saw me as a baby he exclaimed, 'Wow he's going to be a bobby dazzler!' Somehow it just stuck in the family and then got passed on to my friends. I would have preferred Bobby to Dazzle but there it is. I've had to explain it all my life – thank you, Dad!" Dazzle looked towards heaven and put his hands together. "Mind you, it could have been worse. Dad could have said, 'Well, bugger me, he looks just like Winston Churchill!' and I could have been called 'Bugger Me' for ever more."

Mandy laughed out loud. She seemed so out of place amongst the many holiday makers around.

The young females, in the main, wore ill-fitting blouses or crop tops, staggered around on platform shoes, and wore shorts with buttons so strained that if they ever flew off, they would kill someone! The older women were as wrinkled as prunes, had skin the colour of an old purse, and invariably smoked and coughed loudly. Whereas most of the young men in St. Cuthbert's Bay belonged to the baggy jeans, workwear vest or football shirt brigade, and the older men looked as if they'd come straight from the allotment.

Referring to Mandy's earlier comment, Dazzle said, "And I would be delighted to take you out to dinner. Do you like whelks as we're by the seaside?"

"Ugh, I can't imagine anything worse than whelks." Mandy wrinkled her nose up at the thought.

"Don't knock them till you've tried them. The down-and-outs around here love them 'cos they have to chew them from one meal time to the next," countered Dazzle with a huge grin.

"Perhaps a pizza?"

"Whatever you prefer, Mandy. Where are you from?"

"Chelsea."

"I'm afraid we don't have any restaurants that serve anything close to London's fare, but I'll happily meet you at 7.00 p.m. if you'd like and we can savour the best that St. Cuthbert's Bay can offer."

"Can we meet here, please?" asked Mandy as she handed Dazzle one of the wrapped paintings.

"It's a date." He took it from her and picking up his takeaway coffee. "Thank you so much for returning it. I'd better get back to my pitch and thrash a Welsh man if he's negotiated any more BOGOFS, but I'm really looking forward to tonight," he said thoughtfully, and meant it.

"Me too," replied Mandy, smiling up at him.

Dazzle set back off towards the promenade with his painting under his arm and a definite spring in his step. Maybe he should give Yorrie some commission after all.

4

Dazzle had a wonderful time at dinner with Mandy. They laughed and she teased him about Yorrie giving away his paintings as a BOGOF. He reminded her of her introduction – 'I'm Mandy, by the way' – and used the full phrase whenever he asked if she wanted another drink.

Their conversation drifted across many subjects over the course of the meal. They exchanged views on music, books, art, films and favourite cuisine, and there were several connections. She was a pleasure to be with and he couldn't remember when he'd enjoyed anyone's company as much.

As the evening progressed, Dazzle felt comfortable enough to ask what she was doing in St. Cuthbert's Bay.

"I came here to be on my own to think," replied Mandy, with a reflective tone of voice. "When I'm at home I'm delighted to be surrounded by lovely things, but they just make me too contented and lazy to take a risk and start something brand new. When I'm on the beach here there are no distractions, and I can let my mind wander and do lots of 'what if' thinking."

"I can't think of a better reason to spend time by the sea," added Dazzle honestly.

"I'm currently in a job that I love, but it has no future. It's an elderly family run outfit, which they are never going to sell. At present, they are completely dependent upon me for its total turnover, so if I leave, I'll shut the business down overnight. I can't do that to them because they've been very good to me over the years. But I can do the job in my sleep," she said, waving her arms around in protest. "I want some excitement in my life!" She took a drink.

"I want some challenges. I want to feel stretched." She took another drink. "I probably need to start my own business to achieve all those things, but what? The world's my oyster, but my oyster is in a very big sea. I haven't the foggiest idea of the type of business I'd like to start. Is it I.T., sales, HR, design, finance, travel?" She shrugged. "I just don't know; there's too much choice."

Dazzle listened thoughtfully. "Some questions?" he asked.

"Go ahead," said Mandy.

"Do you want to work with people, animals or trees?"

Many cocked her head to one side and pursed her lips thoughtfully. "Oh, I've never really thought about it. I suppose I want to work with people. I thrive on interaction, conversation, company, challenge. I'm OK with animals as long as they are someone else's, and I'm a city girl and like trees but don't want to plant them or cut them down."

"OK," said Dazzle, pleased to have got her thinking. He paused now needing her to narrow them down. "If it's people you want to work with, do you want to work with business people, old people, sick people, or children?"

Mandy shuddered a little at the last two. "This sounds awful, but I struggle to interact with old folk and certainly don't want to work with sick people of any age," she replied, reddening slightly and running her hand through her dark hair. "So, it'd have to be business people for me."

Dazzle nodded, glossing over her obvious embarrassment; he was glad she felt comfortable enough to be brutally honest.

"Do you want to work in a team or on your own?" he asked next, allowing her time to think. He took a long drink of the red wine and popped a bread stick into his mouth while waiting.

"I think I'm much better off working on my own." She added, "That is, unless it's *my* team."

"OK. Do you want to do the same thing every day like a retail shop, or have a new challenge every day, sometimes twice a day?"

She poured herself some more wine while she thought, clearly now understanding the process. "To be faced with a new challenge every day would be utopia." Mandy smiled widely.

"Do you want to work during the day, the night, or on three shifts? Do you want to work inside or outside?"

"That's easy – I'm hopeless if I lose sleep and just can't function properly. Three shifts would be dire for me. However, I love being outside."

"What about the fire service?" suggested Dazzle.

"Like most women, I do like a man in a uniform I have to

say, but I can't stand heights. And they work shifts, don't they?"

"Would you enjoy being a police officer?"

Mandy shook her head. "Not really, again due to the hours. However, I love solving mysteries and problems and my logic thinking is very good. I'm a bit like a dog with a bone when I'm faced with a problem; I'll stay on it till solved. So, if the criminals just burgled or murdered or did whatever they do in the daytime, I'd be fine." She laughed softly.

"How about becoming a paramedic?"

"No. As I said, I'm not good around sick folk and I'm hopeless about blood."

"So, in summary, you want to work with business people, on your own, with a new challenge every day. You want to work during the day, outside, no blood, no heights but solving mysteries to exercise your brain and use your logic thinking every-so-often. Would that be perfect? Have I missed anything?" asked Dazzle.

"No, you've got me to a tee."

"How about your own ice cream van?" ventured Dazzle, tongue in cheek. "You would have to negotiate with caravan site managers around here every day. You would be working on your own, and I am positive you would meet a new challenge every day with the sort of folk who reside here. No heights, no blood and the customers would keep you on your toes."

Mandy frowned at him, no doubt checking if he was joking.

"Well, yes when you break it down like that," she answered, fingering her glass of red wine. "Simple, isn't it?"

"Do you want to carry on a little bit longer?" inquired Dazzle.

"There's more?" asked Mandy, eyebrows raised as she brought her wine glass to her lips.

"One more. If you could meet your younger self, what advice would you give?" he concluded.

Mandy set her glass back on the table and without hesitation answered, "Whatever it is you want to do, just do it now. Don't wait till you are older or for a better time. Just go for it."

Tears pricked Mandy's eyes. Dazzle knew she had just told herself it was OK to follow her dream, to be herself, to put herself first for once. To just go for it.

"So, right now, you want to work on your own, with new challenges every day, outside in the daytime, with business people. That will be 500 guineas for consultancy fees thank you Miss 'Mandy, by the way'. Payable in dinners and wine." He laughed loudly and so did she.

Then, with a serious gaze, Mandy reached out and held one of his hands across the table between the forest of glasses. "Thank you so much, Dazzle. Your simple technique of questions has really helped me this evening."

"Cheers," said Dazzle, raising his glass with his free hand. "I've done nothing. I'm just pleased to have helped you think through the jumble going on in your mind at the moment. Now, to further clear your head, would you like to join me on the beach early tomorrow morning to watch the sun rise over the sea? You London folk probably don't know that there are two tides every day, but there are here, and the light is amazing early in the morning. I'd love to show it to you. As an artist, I think it's a very special time of the day."

There was a long delay before Mandy said anything, her eyes flitting between him and her glass. Then she asked coyly, "Would you help me to get up to see the sun rise with you tomorrow morning, please?"

"Of course! Tell me where you are staying, and I'll be outside bright and early throwing stones at your window to make sure you are up and bouncing ready to sprint down to the beach. I'll even bring some coffee."

Mandy shook her head. "You misunderstand." She paused again, and then asked, "Will you stay with me tonight to make sure I'm up tomorrow morning to go with you to the beach?"

———

Early the next morning, two sets of footprints in the wet sand led from the promenade slipway towards the sea. One dainty woman's set on the left and a man's heavier and wider strides on the right. The prints were close, suggesting hands being held as the feet made their impressions.

Having rolled up their trousers, both early risers found the wet sand to be surprisingly warm for the time of the morning. The tide was as far out as it could be, exposing acres and acres of beach. Worm casts and clumps of seaweed were all that interrupted their view across the bay. The sky was virtually clear in every direction, with only the faintest still white clouds on the horizon to the south. Low rocks and rock-pools bookended the scene to the west of the pair as they walked towards the sea, and high cliffs bookended the scene to the east. The promenade became the backdrop to the bay.

Half way to the sea, the couple were treated to that fresh salty smell, an aroma that one wants to fill one's lungs with. A clean newness to the day. Mandy recounted family holidays that always began in the Morris Minor car with, 'Who will be first to see the sea?' And next, 'Who will be first to smell the sea?' She wistfully stated that the smell meant the holiday had truly started.

As they walked towards the sea Dazzle explained, "The smell of the sea – ozone – was what early doctors misguidedly peddled to combat miasmic theory."

Mandy turned and shrugged her shoulders. "Miasmic?"

"It was a theory that disease and the Black Death were caused by bad smells, so going to places that had good smells – like the seaside – was restorative."

"That sounds silly," she said.

He continued, "To encourage folk, they exaggerated the therapeutic healing properties of the 'bracing sea-side air'. The Victorians and Edwardians were all seduced by the poetic licence of the travel agents and quacks. They flocked here in their thousands to St. Cuthbert's Bay."

"It is a very special smell. The smell of sandcastles and ice cream and laughter and sandwiches," Mandy added, skipping along beside him.

Undeterred, Dazzle continued his scientific explanation, "The smell of the sea is now known to be a cocktail of freshly washed seaweed from recently exposed rock pools, plankton and bacteria – a compound called Dimethyl Sulphide. Even the most verbose and colourful travel agent would be challenged to make the term 'Dimethyl Sulphide' sound inviting. The word 'ozone' had much more of an allure."

"I much prefer my description." She smirked.

As they took in the beauty of the scene, breathing the freshness of the day, the silence was broken abruptly by a Laridae chorus from the high cliffs on the east side of the bay. As more seagulls joined in, the morning chorus became a cacophony, loud enough to startle even locals from their slumbers. Then there was an eerie long silence.

Dazzle and Mandy turned to face the cliffs, holding hands and waiting for the imminent next verse. Suddenly, a twenty-year-old matriarch, on the highest point on the cliff, stretched her white throat up as far as she could reach, then screamed pulsating laughter.

After reverently listening to the solo, the assembled gulls collectively screeched a raucous defiant call as first light broke. Some soared and swooped, screeching close to the gorse-covered cliffs that collected sea fret and dribbled rivulets of water down the cliff's craggy surface onto the beach. The gulls screamed abuse at the wispy clouds that layered above the horizon. Then they screamed at the sea, stuck motionless on the endless turn of the tide. Finally, they screamed for every gull within hearing distance balanced web-footed on the slippery ridge tiles of all the holiday makers' boarding houses and hotels, cajoling them to join their white choir and wake the world.

"Well, if you weren't really awake before, you must be now!" joked Dazzle and smiled at Mandy.

Their smiles morphed into laughter and the couple broke into a run, quickly passing the end of the cliffs to look out to the east. They ran to the water's edge to stand in the shallows. In the centre of the horizon, the first sign of the sun was peeping through the sea; a glowing fire in the sky.

As the show began, Dazzle moved behind Mandy to face the sun, looking over her right shoulder as the sun burst out of the sea, bobbing yellow and red on the fiery horizon.

He circled his arms around her gently. She hugged him to her, and he revelled in their closeness and cats cradled all their fingers.

Mandy whispered, "When I was a little girl and the sun was going down, my dad would make a hissing sound when the hot sun appeared to touch the water."

Dazzle whispered back, "I think every dad did the same thing."

"But my dad did it first!" she corrected him.

Dazzle smiled and gave her a little squeeze.

They stayed on the beach watching the sun rise, in awe of the spectacle and marvelling at the light and colours, the hues and shades. As soon as he had logged a colour in his artist's head, it had already morphed into another colour and another and another. The water started to swirl around their ankles, heading towards the beach. It had risen around their knees by the time they came down to earth, and they sprinted up the beach to stay ahead of the racing tide.

Back at the promenade, Dazzle insisted that an obligatory part of watching the sun rise was a hearty, cooked, full English breakfast. Despite Mandy's protestations that she was on a diet, he led her to a greasy spoon café for early rising building workers. Dazzle laughed as Mandy looked through the steamed windows and turned her nose up, but reluctantly allowed him to lead her inside.

Yet forty minutes later, after sharing a table with painters and decorators, brickies and chippies, scaffolders and lorry drivers, Mandy admitted it had been the best breakfast experience ever.

Dazzle reflected that their banter had been as good as the food, especially when one of the brickies asked where she was from and she replied, "London."

He replied, "Oh, I've got an auntie who lives in London. Perhaps you know her?" The whole table had erupted in laughter.

This was the first day of Mandy's week in St. Cuthbert's Bay but they both knew they wanted to spend more time together. As they finished their mugs of builder's tea, she suggested that Dazzle chose what they should do the next day as a surprise for her, and she would choose what to do on Wednesday as a surprise for him.

On Tuesday, Dazzle insisted on another early start and the two of them went out on a lobster potting expedition. Mandy squealed when one of the crew held up the biggest lobster either of them had ever seen. After spending three hours on a bouncy sea, they were both wet and cold and feeling decidedly unwell. They concluded that it had been an 'interesting' expedition, however, one not to be repeated.

Mandy's choice of date was more elegant. She asked Dazzle to come dressed in his best clothes to a tea dance. All went well until the second dance was announced as a progressive dance. Dazzle's heart sank. The older men in the room were delighted to be dancing with a woman young enough and pretty enough to be their granddaughter, and the elderly ladies were delighted to be guiding a young man around the room who did not smell of urine or 'old raffle prize' aftershave.

The next day, they wandered into the house of slot machines and spent a fortune trying to win back a £1. When they tired of the impossible grab machines, they shook the hand of every one-armed-bandit in the place. The simulated racing cars were next and the competition between them was light-hearted but fierce.

The rest of the week flew by, despite neither being keen to embark on a repeat programme of earlier expeditions. At times they behaved as adolescents, skimming stones and counting the bounces. They ate fish and chips out of newspaper and slept on a rug on the beach in the sunshine after lunch.

Other times they became adults again and just strolled along the cliff top talking about nothing, just happy to be holding each other's hands and smiling. They were just enjoying each other's company and avoiding certain sensitive subjects as neither wanted to hear the answers. Dazzle couldn't remember ever having a better week. Mandy was a lot of fun to be with. He wanted to stay in their bubble for ever.

5

On Friday afternoon, Yorrie was scrutinising the racing paper in his room while listening to his transistor radio, when he heard a loud banging on the front door. No stranger to trouble, he made his way downstairs and casually opened the door, only to be confronted by a big man who immediately reached forward and grabbed him by the front of his pullover.

"Are you Dazzle?" shouted the man.

Yorrie remembered his Welsh valley fighting up-bringing: 'always play for time before you respond'. Time to measure up the opponent and the situation.

"Good Lord, no. And please let go of my pullover. My mam knitted it, and very fond of it I am."

"Where is he then?"

"I don't know, maybe down the beach or out painting somewhere, and please let go of my pullover."

All the while Yorrie was assessing the guy. He was overweight but he stood full on facing him, legs planted wide. If the big guy had been sideways on, life would have been so much harder for Yorrie as his nether region would have been impossible to kick, and it would have been much more difficult to punch him in the face.

Still holding onto Yorrie's pullover, the man yanked him even closer to his face and shouted, "I don't believe you, you scrawny, little, Welsh f–"

Like lightning, Yorrie head butted the man above his left eye.

As he lifted his hands up defensively, Yorrie punched him twice, his bony knuckles connecting with the fleshy parts of the big man's face, once right on the nose and once on his mouth, splitting his top and bottom lip. Finally, he kicked him square on and sent him flying backwards. He landed on the short, wet path on his backside.

Just at that moment, a car pulled up outside the house. Mandy jumped out, followed by Dazzle.

"What the hell's going on?" demanded Dazzle, surveying the scene.

Stepping over the big man, Mandy went straight to Yorrie and held his hands. "I am so sorry, Yorrie, please tell me he didn't hurt you."

"Hurt me? No, Welsh I am. Of course he didn't hurt me. Though he did call me scrawny, which I am a bit, and he called me little, which I am, and he called me Welsh, which I am proud to be, but when he almost called me something else, well, I saw the red mist of the dragon's breath and had to teach him some manners, didn't I?"

The big guy groaned, blood streaming from his nose and mouth all down his white tee shirt. "What about me?"

"I'll talk to you later," snapped Mandy.

Dazzle frowned. "Do you know him? Who the hell is he?" he asked.

"He's... he's my husband," replied Mandy, dropping Yorrie's hands and looking away.

"Oh. You didn't say," said Dazzle quietly.

"Well, you didn't ask," she shot back immediately.

Dazzle nodded, stepped over the man and headed inside the house.

"Help him into Mandy's car," Dazzle said to Yorrie, without looking back.

"His nose and his lip I hit, not his legs. He can get hisself into the car," declared Yorrie, following Dazzle and closing the door behind them.

———

The rest of the summer of '94 dragged on. Every week was long and lonely. Dazzle constantly castigated himself for not asking Mandy the simple question of whether she was married or not.

Perhaps he just hadn't wanted to know or, more to the truth, he already knew and hadn't wanted to have it confirmed. But he just couldn't get her out of his mind, day or night.

Autumn came and went, followed by dreadfully wet winter. Mandy gradually faded from the forefront of his mind and life returned to its former dreary normal for Dazzle. And Yorrie.

In spring, new artists in rose-coloured glasses arrived and swelled the number of offerings on the promenade, forcing older, more life-bruised artists to take other jobs to make ends meet. Dazzle wondered how long before he joined the battered egos with a second job.

Two long summers of mixed weather later, on an early Sunday morning in June '96 , the weather was cloudy, but thankfully not raining. The wind was gentle, so Dazzle's tenting expertise to protect his art was not required. Over the course of the morning, a steady flow of customers called in to see his display and he sold two paintings. It was a good day.

Towards midday, an elderly gentleman came to his pitch who wanted to tell his story, as so often is the case with lonely, old people. "Did you know that I was once a water-colour painter and won several national competitions? Sadly, my eyesight is failing and now my brushes are hung up for good."

Patiently engaged with the gentleman, Dazzle felt the wind beginning to spring up, but as the conversation developed, he started to become more anxious to secure the waterproofing over his paintings. However, he was also conscious of the man's loneliness and Yorrie hadn't returned with more stock yet. Politeness won in the end and the conversation with the old gentleman continued. A few moments of his time was a small cost to pay.

Suddenly, the man's hat blew off. It turned over and over as it bounced along the promenade.

Dazzle spotted Yorrie on his way back and rushed off in pursuit of the hat, calling out to his tenant to erect the polythene over the paintings. The gentleman followed, also in pursuit of his hat. Ten minutes later the man and his hat were reunited, and many thanks were offered to Dazzle.

By this time, the wind had picked up even more. It was quite blustery, and Dazzle raced back to his pitch. Yorrie had lost the first sheet of polythene over the promenade wall, and it danced and rolled along the emptying beach. Dazzle sent him to chase after it. The remaining awning, now in tatters, was flapping in the wind. Rain was imminent. A lady who had been looking at Dazzle's paintings offered to help. Luckily, she caught one end of the awning before it disappeared in the wake of the polythene. Between them they wrestled the flapping awning and clipped it to the frame.

An enormous gust then ripped the awning off the frame, pinging crocodile clips in all directions. The customer and Dazzle became wrapped in the flapping awning, and Dazzle slipped and fell to the ground. The lady tried to catch Dazzle but wasn't strong enough to hold him, and slipped on the wet awning too, landing next to him.

Two other artists, seeing the dilemma, ran to help save his paintings, covering them with a spare waterproof. Just as suddenly as the wind had sprung up, it dropped to nothing. And all was quiet again.

Dazzle untangled himself slowly from the voluminous awning and as soon as he was free, he thanked the two other artists for saving his paintings. He then turned his attention to the customer who was now on her knees, but struggling to stand up.

He helped her up but one of her shoes had fallen off in the process. Dazzle retrieved it and thanked the woman profusely for her help. There was a long pause as the lady sat upon a nearby bench and returned her shoe to her foot, panting from her exertions.

Once she had her breath back, she asked, "Are you the artist? Because they're very good."

"I am. And thank you."

"If you are the artist, then what's the signature on the paintings?"

Dazzle was taken aback.

"Well, they're my initials, of course."

"Which are?"

Dazzle frowned, unsure why she was asking. "The large seascape is signed D. J. Q. 1990, and the smaller one has D. J. Q. 1991 on it. My name is Dazzle John Quill."

The woman smiled. "So, it is you, Dazzle! I thought I recognised your voice when I heard you speak to the older gentleman, but I couldn't place it. You've changed a bit but haven't we all? Now I can see it is still you."

Dazzle looked at the woman, wondering how she knew him. "Have we met before? Have you bought any of my paintings before? Are you an artist too?"

"I'll give you two clues: art class in the 70s."

The penny dropped and Dazzle became so excited he could hardly speak, his words jumbled out.

"Miss Cartwright? Good grief! Wow, how lovely to see you. You haven't changed a bit," he complimented kindly. "I should have known from your voice but because of the wind, I couldn't hear you properly."

"Oh, I have changed, and you are still the same charmer you always were in school, Dazzle Quill."

"The last time we saw each other must have been nineteen years ago! What are you doing here?" He sat alongside her on the bench.

"I run a small art gallery in London and every so often I go hunting for top of the range paintings to sell in my gallery. I must confess I was getting a bit disheartened as I walked along the promenade, till I saw your display. I should have known." She pointed to the large seascape. "May I buy this one myself for your asking price? I'll take another back to London and sell it for you, if you'd like. I'll promise you £295, and I'll keep the rest. What do you think?"

Dazzle blinked in surprise. 'OK!" he said and laughed. "Hey, what are you doing for dinner tonight?" he asked without thinking, then immediately regretted being so eager. She might be with her family or going back to London straightaway.

She shrugged. "Nothing."

"May I take you out to the best restaurant St. Cuthbert's Bay has to offer please, Miss Cartwright. It would be so good to catch up."

"I'd be delighted to go out for dinner with you, Dazzle. Shall we meet here later? And please call me Susan, although I am Miss Cartwright to the students I still teach."

"Great. I'll look forward to it, Susan," said Dazzle, still in disbelief at the surprising turn of events. He chuckled to himself. It was funny how life unfolded sometimes.

———

Dinner began as a slightly stilted affair, but the wine accelerated the breaking down of barriers. Dazzle and Susan kept remembering incidents from when they were both at the school, which caused bursts of laughter.

"Did the music teacher really make Veronica Mablethorpe pregnant? Are they still together?" fished Dazzle, setting down his wine glass.

"I couldn't possibly say," said Susan before taking a large drink. She smirked over the rim of her glass at him. "But yes," she confirmed. "I think they now are grandparents."

"Who in your form burnt a hole in my coat with a magnifying glass?" she challenged. "You can say now!"

"I couldn't possibly tell you..." teased Dazzle. "But it was Dick Tench who sat in the front row."

"Do you know what ever happened to Donnie, Big Colin and Dan? They were always together and real troublemakers," asked Susan

"Oh, they did OK. They formed a small company with Donnie as the brains and they all became very rich very quickly, somehow." Dazzle knowingly tapped his nose. "Then they did one job too many and ended up in the nick. The Scrubs, I think. A few others are dead now too. Chemical heads, drugs and motorbike accidents."

The conversation ranged far and wide covering the best books each had read, what music was special to them and why, what tastes they each had in wine, and the different cuisines they enjoyed most. Each wanted to know what holidays the other had been on, and when Dazzle posed the question about who Susan would most like to meet from history, they knew it was late.

However, the wine flowed again, and their laughter became louder. Neither wanted the evening to end.

Once dinner was finally over and the bar staff were drumming their fingers on the bar wanting to clear the last table in the restaurant, Susan asked if she could see some of Dazzle's other work. He agreed, and they strolled back to his tiny, terraced house, chatting as they went. Susan slid her arm into his and gave him a squeeze as they walked and reminisced. He was having the best evening and felt a million dollars.

Dazzle was a methodical character and had kept some paintings for himself through the decades, so once in his lounge, Susan flicked through his art, stopping to admire some and turn her nose up at others as she viewed his changing styles. Dazzle just watched, barely believing his luck that his Miss Cartwright was in his home after all this time.

After looking through everything, she started again at the beginning. "When you were a pupil of mine, I saw in you real talent, real flair. Now that wasn't surprising compared with the rest of the class who couldn't even use a road sweeper's brush! But I wasn't comparing you with them, I was comparing you with other watercolour artists in my evening classes and you were already up there with the best. You had something, you saw colours and shapes that many did not. I was impressed by your expressiveness, your imaginative perspectives, an over-boldness in your brush strokes. However, you were clumsy in your composition and used some juvenile techniques – as expected for someone your age. Behind all that, your real talent was obvious."

Dazzle listened in awe with his eyes open wide. He shook his head, flattered by her compliments.

"Luckily, you have dated all your work so it's easy to follow your development journey. You evolved strangely in your late twenties, showing much more anger and needing to exert much more control in your meticulous choice and use of brush sizes. Darker colours and much more structure dominated this period. Maybe the time coincided with when you were trying to teach art and didn't have any control over your pupils or satisfaction in your life, or faith in your future. It all came out in your art. You magnified a sad time in your life, in paint."

Dazzle nodded in agreement. It really had been a sad time in his life.

"In your thirties, you achieved more expression. You became looser with your hand movements, shown in longer sweeps of the brushes and clearer curves, and you became more expressive with colour, depicting a calmer, more confident artist. If I'm not mistaken you were enjoying your art more? Am I right?"

Dazzle was impressed with his former teacher's analysis. "You're right, I was in a better place and even I could see improvements in my work. I was never completely satisfied, but it was better. What do you think of my most recent works?"

"Softer brush strokes and more dynamic application techniques demonstrate that, right now, you're exploring atmosphere, light and the movement of clouds. You interpret the changing play of light on water well." She smiled wistfully. "This is probably the hardest image to portray: mist, rain and the flow of water baffle even the most skilful of artists. Now you're comfortable using energetic swirling strokes to depict water movement. You've lost the desire to try to paint images but are focussed on capturing the essence of a scene for the viewer to interpret."

"Wow," said Dazzle softly.

"I'm right, aren't I?"

"You're spot on, but I've never been able to put it into words."

Dazzle listened as she interpreted more of his life as an artist, cleverly reading the paintings as if she had been there watching over his shoulder through the years. Re-captivated, he watched her every movement, remembering the unconscious flick of her hair and her hand gestures. In one evening, he had been transported back to when he was seventeen and so enthralled by her.

As she was tidying his paintings in the silence that followed, she moved a spare easel, and a rolled canvas fell to the floor. He jumped to retrieve it first but was too late. She spread the canvas on the table and turned on the angle poise light for a better view. The painting was of her relaxing on a settee reading a book, the half-light of a window to her left and a hazy door to her right. She looked at the date; Dazzle had been seventeen when he painted it. She looked up at him and he reddened. He knew he had captured her contentedness; it exuded from the picture. There was a peacefulness in its composition, and she could no doubt feel the warmth and love in every brush stroke. A calmness which he believed was her natural demeanour shone from the page.

"You kept this one of me all these years?" she whispered.

Slightly embarrassed, he looked away.

"Why?" she asked gently.

Dazzle sighed. There was no point denying it now. "Isn't it obvious? I was completely in love with you."

"You sweetie! It's very good. How did you know then that I liked to read in the evenings?"

"Because it fitted with every mental image I had of you. I tried to imagine your routine at home on your own. Schoolwork first followed by a sensible salad, maybe some music on in the background. In the absence of company, you would probably flick through a magazine as you ate. When all the jobs were done you would pick up the book which you had left perched on the arm of the settee the previous night."

"Did you paint any other pictures of me in other poses or other clothes?" she teased.

"No, you were too important to me to try to guess what you looked like underneath your clothes. I never want to paint anything that I hadn't actually seen."

"I never knew," she said, gazing at the painting again.

"Yes, you did," argued Dazzle, brave from the wine and knowing the gap in their ages had shrunk to nothing now.

"Well, OK, apart from your spots, I did think you were by far the best looking in the school."

"Thanks."

Susan turned to face him and perched on the back of the two-seater sofa. "After you left school, I did fantasise occasionally of lying naked on your bed as you painted me. But then, in the fantasy, your parents came home unexpectedly, and all hell broke loose. So, I quickly put that fantasy out of my head and came down to earth. But I have thought of you many times since then and wondered what became of you. I so hoped you hadn't given up painting."

"I wondered what had happened to you too. Where did you live? Had you met someone? Were you happy?"

The atmosphere in the tiny lounge had grown serious; tinged with the weight of Dazzle's unrequited school crush. The music behind their words had evolved subtly over the evening, from gentle oboe and cello notes accompanying delightful memories, to a slightly faster rhythm of infatuation. Now a bumble bee crescendo mirrored the intensity of the growing attraction between them.

Susan smiled sadly. "What happened to me? Nothing really." She looked around the tiny room as she talked. "I stayed at the school for another fifteen dreadful years, but in the background, I developed my evening teaching classes. Along the way, I fell in love and got married. Unfortunately, it didn't last. He wanted children but it just never happened for us, so we parted. Chemistry I suppose." Dazzle registered the sadness on her face as she recounted the unhappy time. She continued, "My ex-husband found someone who could give him what he wanted and now he has three lovely children. I'm happy for him. I've been on my own ever since."

Dazzle moved closer and looked into her eyes. Their heads tilted. The bumblebee music restarted, becoming louder. After sensing each other's breath, their lips had barely touched when... the brightness of the main light nearly blinded them!

In bounced Yorrie, instantly bringing them both back to earth.

"Oh, my God. Sorry, I am. I didn't know you had company, Dazzle. You never have company!"

Susan and Dazzle quickly moved apart as Yorrie fought to rectify his intrusion.

"Hey, I'll be off to bed then. 'Up the wooden hill' as my mam used to say. Sorry to disturb, shall I turns the light back off? Anyway, I'll see you both in the morning then. Well, no, I didn't mean that. I didn't mean nothing. It came out all wrong. I was just being pol–"

"Shut up, Yorrie," said Dazzle.

"Right you are. Off upstairs I'm going. On my way. On my way."

6

Two days later, Dazzle appeared back at his house with Susan. In the very short time they had been together, they had become close. Very close. They had many years of catching up to do.

She was collecting a painting to take back to London to sell for him, as well as the one she had already paid him for. Susan had made Dazzle an offer better than anything he could ever have imagined: she would collect a new painting every month to sell in London. He would be paid twice what he could get in St. Cuthbert's Bay.

Yorrie helped load the packaged paintings into her car but had the good sense to disappear before she left.

Susan gave Dazzle a quick peck on his cheek. "Don't be sad, I'll be back in four weeks so stay warm for me."

Then she got in her car and drove away, and Dazzle's life became instantly quiet again.

After a reasonable length of time had elapsed, Yorrie came downstairs and made some tea for them both. Dazzle excitedly explained his and Susan's arrangement with the paintings. Yorrie thought about it, rose out of his chair and patted Dazzle on his shoulder.

"That's a really amazing deal, Daz. I'm very happy for you. I think you are on your way up to fame and fortune. But as my old dad used to say: 'Don't sell the pelt till you've shot the bear.'"

"Shut up, Yorrie," snapped Dazzle.

———

The next two weeks dragged on, and life became ten times worse for Dazzle. He'd had a taste of what life could be like and what had he been left with – just Yorrie and Yorrie's dad's bloody sayings. Susan was everything he had imagined she would be: thoughtful, considerate and gentle. She hadn't let go of him since their first night together. Not clingy but serious, sensitive and warm. Already he missed her terribly.

After a particularly bad Sunday, Yorrie noticed the obvious drop in Dazzle's spirits.

"I've got a cracking idea," said Yorrie. "Hows about we go out for a couple of pints tonight and then call in for fish and chips on the way home? I cleaned a few more cars last Saturday so it's my treat."

Dazzle thought about it. "Yes, why not? I could do with cheering up a bit. Let's go now before I change my mind."

Yorrie selected the local high-end boozer that had a juke box, and they settled in. While Yorrie was at the bar, Dazzle went to choose some lively music to cheer up the dreary Sunday atmosphere.

A few seconds later, Dazzle saw Yorrie being dragged over the bar by his lapels before the soles of his desert boots disappeared too. A huge commotion ensued and a second bartender rushed in to join the melee. Glasses and bottles were broken and the glass splintered everywhere. The noise was deafening.

Dazzle ran around the bar to drag the two bartenders off Yorrie and immediately became part of the fight. Now it was two on two. Another man, presumably the bar owner, rushed in to sort out the troublemakers. He wrenched the bartenders off Yorrie then frog-marched him through the quiet bar and threw him down the short flight of steps onto the street. Turning back, he set his sights on the second supposed troublemaker – Dazzle himself.

Despite all protestations, the bar owner was not in the mood for explanations. He grabbed Dazzle by his arm, marched him through the bar and pushed him outside too. Dazzle landed on top of Yorrie at the bottom of the steps. The bar owner's parting words were, "Now f*** off the pair of you and don't come back. In fact, you're both barred for three months!"

The two of them helped each other up and went to sit on a bench on the promenade to assess their wounds. Yorrie had a large cut above his eye and probably a broken nose. Dazzle had been in the fight the least time but sustained a black eye and maybe a broken finger, fortunately on his left hand.

"What in God's name did you say to the bartender?" asked Dazzle, nursing his hand.

"I asked him for two drinks and two packets of crisps, that's all." Yorrie shrugged his shoulders.

"You must have said something else. Tell me exactly," demanded Dazzle, stroking his wounded eye.

"I said, 'May I have a pint of bitter for my friend and I'm feeling in a Spanish mood, so I'd like a Penis Colada and two packets of crisps, please.' Then I seemed to be flying."

Dazzle shook his head and looked at Yorrie disbelievingly. "The bartender is gay and probably thought you were tasking the pee. It's not a 'Penis Colada', it's a 'Pina Colada'. Literally, it means strained pineapple. Pineapple is called pina in Spain because they think it looks like a pine cone."

"Oh, bollocks. That explains everything then. I went on a cheap holiday to Spain with some of my mates years ago, and they told me it was called a Penis Colada. Every time I ordered one, I got invited to some seedy club or other by the bartender when his bar closed, but it always ended the same, with my new friend the bartender trying to puts his hand down my shorts! I got into so many fights on that holiday. My mates are a real set of bastards!"

———

Since Susan had come into his life Dazzle had felt a huge lift. Even Yorrie began to notice improvements in his landlord's level of his patience with visitors to his Sunday promenade display. Despite Dazzle missing Susan and her seriousness more than he would say, he was happier, probably because in his mind he felt there was a real possibility of a lasting relationship – his greatest wish.

This positive change in his behaviour was noticed by all as he had far more time for customers' lack of decision-making capacity. He was more cheerful with them, and happy to pass the time of day with them, even if they didn't buy anything. Unfortunately, he didn't know many of their names and so gave them nicknames based upon something in their dress, manner or spending potential. He only shared these names with Yorrie so they both knew who they were talking about. The silliness brightened their Sundays.

For instance, there was Miss Bumfuzzled. A dumpy, busy lady with unkempt, seaweed hair tied back with a scarf, who always toted a well-worn rucksack. Bordering on dressing as a vagrant, she had a stoop, which was only corrected by a well-worn, twisted, hazel walking stick.

Through thick spectacles, she browsed Dazzle's paintings, peering closely at each one. Always in a hurry, which added an element of mystery to her, she tut-tutted at every price. Being short, she had a habit of shuffling along his display and pushing in front of other potential customers, who smiled at her.

"Poor old soul," they whispered to each other.

Dazzle looked past her appearance and they had many arty conversations. He came to the conclusion that she was intelligent, empathetic and rebelliously eccentric. Her dress code gave her the gift of anonymity, allowing her to navigate the world on her terms. Her desire to remain unobtrusive was her stance against materialism and vanity. As someone who appeared to love art he wondered if she also enjoyed the creativity and adventure of adopting different personas on her own life's canvas. Perhaps it was her way of displaying her artistic expression.

Dazzle concluded she was living her life in different chosen narratives. Her facial expression was always downcast, avoiding eye contact, however, when she spoke to him about his work, her face lit up with genuine interest and warmth.

Dazzle was fond of Miss Bumfuzzled. Her visits were always a delight.

If she ever bought one of his paintings, she paid in copper coins, small silver, £1 coins and the odd £5 note. She once offered a gold watch in part payment, but he declined. In hindsight, perhaps he should have taken the watch, for a few years later he discovered her husband Willie ran the only local ice cream van in the town, hence all the change. Locally his van was called *Chilly Willie's Bank*: a veritable mobile pawnbroker where everything had a price, everything was obtainable, and he also sold ice cream.

Mrs. Fitzwallerby's visits were enjoyed more than most. A delightfully elegant lady from a different era, she spoke beautifully and pronounced every letter of every word. She was full of fun and joked with Dazzle and Yorrie.

Knowledgeable about art, she could hold her own in a discussion. Despite being a larger lady, she appeared not to take steps but to glide along the promenade, giving the impression of being motorised. Dazzle and Yorrie agreed that, in her youth, Mrs. Fitzwallerby had probably been a ballroom dancer.

In clothes of yesteryear, she wore a long skirt nearly down to the ground even in the summertime. In the winter her coat was long, of high quality, and trimmed with fur. Her make-up was tasteful, she was always hatless, and her hair was tied carefully in a neat but severe bun. She appeared to like paintings of scenes that could be viewed from the promenade and was always happy and smiling.

Both Dazzle and Yorrie believed she brightened their Sundays. However, as soon as she was well out of earshot, they linked arms and sang:

"So stately as a galleon she swept across the floor,

Doing the Military Two-step as in the days of yore.

So gay the band, so giddy the sight, for evening dress is a must.

But the zest goes out of a waltz when... you dance it bust to bust." *

And they bumped chests and fell about laughing.

Miss Sensible Shoes was also a welcome customer. So called because she always wore women's lace-up brogues, even in the summertime. She was an infrequent buyer but always cheerful and full of stories. She was the only customer with whom Dazzle and Yorrie shared their coffee.

They guessed there was some link with the military for her manner belied a level of authority. She was just a lovely, delightful person they were always pleased to see.

One Sunday she arrived earlier than usual carrying a shopping basket. When settled, she unwrapped the parcel to reveal a thermos flask of coffee, three china plates and a fruit loaf.

She turned to Yorrie, "Do you know what this is?"

Yorrie smelled the fruit loaf, and his eyes lit up. "It's Bara Brith."

"Bendigedig, which means wonderful," said Yorrie. "I haven't tasted Bara Brith since I left home."

Dazzle thought he saw a tear well up in his tenant's eye.

------

* Many apologies to the late Joyce Grenfell for her *Old Time Dancing* poem referencing the shortage of males on the dance floor.

"And do you know what Bara Brith means?" asked Miss Sensible shoes as she unpacked butter and knives.

"Of course I do – speckled bread," stated Yorrie.

Three thick slices were cut, spread with butter and served. They ate in silence.

Afterwards, Yorrie gave Miss Sensible Shoes a peck on her cheek. "You've made my day," he declared.

"The coffee and fruit loaf are because you two make my day whenever I come here. It's my birthday today and I can't think of two nicer guys I'd like to share it with. Oh, and by the way, I'm a Gog too," she said.

"Never? You're really a Gog?" replied the astonished Yorrie.

"Yes."

"A Gog?" enquired a very confused Dazzle, shaking his head.

Yorrie turned to Dazzle and explained. "A Gog is short for Gogledd. In Welsh, it means north, so someone from North Wales."

The two Gogs set about comparing notes about home. Dazzle wondered how long it would be before they found out they were second cousins or whatever. An interested customer then caught Dazzle's eye, so he went to serve them, leaving Yorrie singing *Happy Birthday* in Welsh, he assumed.

Coffee and Welsh cakes or Bara Brith became a regular break treat on Sundays, and on very cold days some welcome whisky also appeared in the coffee.

———

Another reasonably interesting customer was Mr. Papadopoulos, who was always accompanied by Bruno, his Bernese Mountain dog. They were irregular visitors to Dazzle's display, but Mr. P. did purchase occasionally.

Unfortunately for Dazzle, Bruno had been fitted with a canine clock and when the dog considered an inordinate amount of time had been wasted talking, he continued the walk, despite the protestations of Mr. P. being dragged behind.

On this particular Sunday, Dazzle believed he was close to selling Mr. P. a painting, so suggested Yorrie might like to take Bruno on a short walk, enabling him to complete the sale. Yorrie nearly passed out at the thought, reminding Dazzle of his glass back.

Ignoring him completely, Mr. P. handed Bruno's lead to very pale Yorrie, and explained that if he spoken to the dog with authority, he was very obedient. Unfortunately, dogs were not allowed on the beach in the summer months and Yorrie was unsure about walking him along the long promenade. He protested vehemently, in vain.

Eventually, he set off at a trot, Yorrie at 120 lbs holding on to one end of the lead, and 140 lbs of mountain dog connected to the other.

Dazzle returned to the potential sale. Mr. P. ummed and ahhed, explaining that he was trying to imagine the painting in his house.

Dazzle suggested, "How about you pay for the picture and take it home. If it is not exactly what you want, you can bring it back and I'll refund the full amount?"

———

Further up the promenade, holidaymakers were already hanging over the sea wall, pointing and laughing as a Bernese Mountain dog, who couldn't read the *Dogs are Banned* notices, with one vacant end to its lead, snaked between the heavily populated deckchairs with a lady's bikini top in his mouth. The owner of the bikini top was attempting to chase after the dog, beside herself, and only partially succeeding in covering her modesty.

Two male beach attendants were also hotly in pursuit, probably each hoping to reach the woman before they reached the dog. Another man half-heartedly following, presumably the woman's husband, didn't look capable of catching or confronting the giant dog.

And then there was Yorrie, coming up the rear. He was trying to use his most assertive voice to command Bruno to stop, despite being a trifle squeaky at times, and following it up with expletives in Welsh, about dogs in general.

Bruno suddenly dropped the bikini top and put his nose in the air. Yorrie believed this was his opportunity to pounce on the dog, as did the other pursuers no doubt, but Bruno had other ideas for it became clear he had been attracted by the odours of a nearby picnic. Like lightning, he collected a mouthful of chicken breasts off the colourful blanket and raced off again between the deck chairs, chewing and swallowing the food as he ran further.

Full of chicken, Bruno suddenly stopped in the most crowded part of the beach, turned around and around, arched his back and prepared to have a huge dump on the golden sand. Folk on all sides were trying to shoo him away, but once he'd started, he could only stop when he had completely finished. Like all well-brought-up dogs, once his ablutions were complete, he cleaned his four paws by kicking sand out behind him, all over shrieking holidaymakers, blankets and deckchairs.

This pause in the chase allowed the partially clothed woman to restore her modesty, and the beach attendants to catch up and hold Bruno's collar. They waited one either side for Yorrie to resume his place on the lead. Only all three men holding the panting dog kept him still, but catching him appeared to be nothing compared to the ordeal suffered by furious holidaymakers. Their shouts rose to a crescendo; the smell was now over-powering.

"Do you have a poo bag?" yelled one of the irate beach attendants.

"Poo bag?" shouted Yorrie above the angry crowd. "Poo bag? That lot will take a f***ing bin liner." He eyed the huge, steaming heap.

"Well, you'll have to clean it up somehow," demanded the other beach attendant. "You can't leave it there!"

Yorrie looked around for something, any sort of receptacle, anything. He lurched forward and snatched a large bucket and spade off a child who was carefully carrying water from the sea probably to his sandcastle's moat further up the beach, oblivious to the noise and crowds.

Despite the chorus of dissent around him, Yorrie emptied the water out of the child's bucket and started loading the poo into it. The child began wailing.

A man, presumably the child's father, quickly arrived and demanded Yorrie buy the howling child another bucket and spade. And an ice cream... for them both. And one for his wife.

Once Yorrie had cleared up the poo, the beach attendants calmed the crowd while they held onto Bruno's lead and collar. Yorrie breathed a sigh of relief, glad the incident was over. If only.

Suddenly, the old lady whose picnic with her four grandchildren had been ruined by Bruno, caught up with Yorrie and started hitting him clumsily with her handbag for allowing his dog onto the beach in the summertime. This continued all the way to the promenade, and Yorrie was only allowed to break away to buy the replacement bucket and spade for the wailing child.

Then he came back out to the ice-cream van to fulfil his second apology, and one detachment of the enemy was finally placated. He bought five more ice creams to make up for the old lady's demolished picnic, and the second detachment of the enemy was placated. The final enemy was the beach attendant duo. Yorrie bought two more ice creams for them, but they had learned a thing or two by now. They requested hundreds and thousands of coloured sprinkles at an extra cost, a double flake at an extra cost, and chocolate sauce at an extra cost. The third enemy was placated.

As he noisily licked the sauce off his raspberry ice cream, the senior beach attendant commented, "And don't think you're leaving that bucket of poo here. You'll have to take it home!"

Mr. Papadopoulos arrived just at that moment carrying a packaged painting, which he protected from the melee. Bruno was so pleased to see him he wagged his tail, banging it loudly against the angry ice cream vendor's van. He'd clearly had a great time, but the ice cream vendor was not impressed. Mr. P. was profuse in his thanks to Yorrie for looking after the dog. He vigorously shook Yorrie's hand and enquired whether he would like to take Bruno out for regular walks as he had established such a rapport with him in such a short time. It took all of Yorrie's willpower not to swear.

A completely frazzled Yorrie finally returned to Dazzle at the end of the promenade.

A waiting Dazzle snapped, "Where the hell have you been? I'm busting for a pee. You were only supposed to keep the bloody dog occupied till Mr. Popo, Popolol, or whatever his name is, paid for the frigging painting, not walk its canine legs off."

"I– I– I was..." stuttered Yorrie, pointing limply at the beach.

"And what's that God awful smell?" Dazzle clasped his hand over his nose as he clocked what Yorrie was carrying. "What are you doing with a bucket full of dog poo?"

"Don't ask! Right? Don't f***ing ask," snapped back Yorrie, pointing his finger at Dazzle.

7

Regular as clockwork, Susan came back to St. Cuthbert's Bay.

During July, August and September, she descended on the doorstep every four weeks with a bundle of cash for Dazzle. Arriving at about 6.00 p.m. on a Friday, she then drove Dazzle to her hotel so she could have a shower after her drive from London, and then the two of them headed out for dinner.

The next time Yorrie saw either of them was about 6.00 p.m. on Sunday evening. Susan always left it late to miss the traffic heading back into London. Yorrie didn't mind for it meant he could watch what he liked on the TV all weekend. Dazzle and Susan seemed close and happy, but Susan's visits flew by, and they were always followed by a real downturn in Dazzle's spirits.

Then one Wednesday during October, she sent him a letter. Yorrie snuck a look at it too.

The letter read:

Dear Dazzle,

So sorry, darling. I have an exhibition opportunity for my work, and the date is our next weekend. As you know only too well, you don't pass up this sort of opportunity to display your art. I'll have to stay on in London that weekend. I'll miss you terribly. Please could you post me your latest watercolour to the following P.O. box number: P.O. Box 20779715, Jury Street, Chelsea. Loved the last one. I'll settle up next time I see you.

Susan xx

Dazzle's mood went down and down. He met Yorrie's offers to go out on the town to cheer him up with, "What, after last time? You must be joking! Unless there's fighting and being barred from the only decent pub in town involved, you don't think you've had a proper night out, do you? By the way, how is your nose? I still can't move my left ring finger even now. So, thank you, Yorrie, but I'm fine staying here."

Then he parcelled up his latest painting and sent it off to Susan at the P. O. box number in London.

Yorrie mumbled to himself, "God, I've got another five weeks to puts up with this. Never mind, at least I have tea with Miss Sensible Shoes, whose real name is Miss Deborah Archer, to look forward to, and her amazing Bara Brith."

One wet November Sunday, the forecast suggested the weather would be biblical rain. So, Deborah invited Yorrie and Dazzle over to her house for tea as there would be no promenade meeting opportunity. Over the previous few weeks, she and Yorrie had met regularly and enjoyed each other's company. Her Welsh was not sufficiently fluent to hold conversations, but she kept trying, much to Yorrie's amusement. Anyone else's cooking was a bonus in Yorrie's life, but homemade cakes were a real treat. Dazzle had the good sense not to be a gooseberry and courteously declined the invitations, but Yorrie always brought home some Welsh cakes for Dazzle.

Yorrie returned home from their afternoon and recounted the day's events. He shared with Dazzle their teatime conversation.

"Deborah asked me what I did for a profession. I explained that I was the first of my family to ever go to university. They had been so proud when I started work in a land surveyor's office then as a real cartographer in a local authority."

"Was she impressed?" asked Dazzle. Yorrie could tell he was only feigning interest.

"I think so. I told her I loved having power over irate farmers, fought passionately for the rights-of-way of walkers, and that I revelled in confrontations with cowboy builders who would try to grease my palm in order to move footpaths in the dead of night to suit their building plans. Unsuccessfully, I might add. I told her most of all I loved the cut and thrust of court room battles about ancient rights of way."

"Wow, I didn't know you did that either. You probably went way up in her expectations."

Yorrie eventually arrived at the crux of his story. "Gets this though – Deborah was a Chief Superintendent in the police in a couple of counties! I was flabbergasted at the revelation, I was!"

Dazzle raised his eyebrows at the news, and commented, "I can imagine her in uniform."

Yorrie went on to explain how Deborah had told him how tough life had been as the only female Chief Superintendent, and some of the taunting she had to endure. "However," said Yorrie, "it had been her criminal clean-up rates that spoke the loudest in the early 90s. Apparently, she built a very effective team who didn't always play to the rules, but they were way out in front in the clean-up league. She could silence a whole gaggle of whispering, testosterone fired male superintendents by asking, 'How's your clean-up rate coming on?'"

"How long did she stay in the police?" asked Dazzle.

"Thirty years!" said Yorrie. "After that, she'd had enough and retired on a full pension, so she did."

"Not sure I'd want to be in a relationship with an ex-senior police officer," said Dazzle. "I'd worry every time I did something wrong. And don't forget all the car washing and bar work you do is cash-in-hand, and you've never heard of income tax, have you? Mind you, there may be an upside. Does she still have her handcuffs? You'd better watch your step."

"She's not like that at all," snapped Yorrie.

———

The Wednesday before the next weekend Susan was due to visit, Dazzle received another note.

Yorrie groaned to himself as Dazzle stomped up the stairs. He retrieved the scrumpled-up letter from the bin and read:

Hi Dazzle,

Thank you for your latest painting. I fear I will have to up your rate if you continue getting better like this. Your other paintings are flying off the walls. Would it be possible to do two paintings this month, darling? I have a customer who wants to be there to open them when they arrive? If he buys them as quickly as he bought the last one, I will up your rate to £400 each. Hope that's OK?

By the way, my exhibition was a real success! I managed to get two commissions out of it, so I'll be too busy for our next scheduled weekend together. So sorry, but you can't pass up commissions, can you? Especially when the customer is so demanding!

I miss you very much, and I promise to make it up to you when we next meet.

Please post the paintings to the same P.O. box.

Lots of love to Yorrie.
All my love,
Your Susan xx

After four weeks of painting day and night, Dazzle finally showed Yorrie his new painting. As he was wrapping them both carefully, Yorrie suggested including a polite notice reminding Susan about the payment. Dazzle agreed, and once written, read his note aloud:

My dear Susan,
Hope you are well and the commissions are going as you would like. Herewith enclosed are the two paintings as requested, one of the bay and the other of the cliffs on the north side of the bay. I hope they are what you wanted.
If you could see your way clear to putting a cheque in the post it would help enormously, as I am struggling to paint for sale here, as well as paint for you. It would also stop Yorrie grumbling about queueing up at a food bank for homeless people. I think about £1500 should cover the last four paintings.
When are you going to invite me to your gallery? I would so like to see what you have created and to watch you in action selling to the general public.
Nothing new ever happens here apart from bumping into old art teachers, so I miss you terribly.
Much love,
Dazzle
xxxxxxxxxxxxxxx

Yorrie gave him the thumbs up and told him to post it with the paintings straightaway.

However, two further months passed without Susan returning to St. Cuthbert's Bay. According to her letters, she wasn't well in December, and she'd had to go to a funeral in January.

Dazzle was becoming unbearable to live with yet continued to send two paintings a month, despite not receiving any more money. Yorrie and Dazzle estimated that Susan now owed Dazzle £4,100, so Yorrie believed he had to do something.

His efforts to cheer his landlord up were like lighting a fuse. When he said, "Cheer up, Daz. As my old dad used to say: 'If you're on the right side of the grass when you wake up in the morning, it's going to be a good day!'"

Dazzle's response was, "Yorrie, shut the f*** up, OK?"

Yorrie's answer to the problem was to discuss it with Deborah. They met at her house for tea and cake, and they talked over all the little bits of information surrounding the situation.

"Do you think Susan is telling him the truth?" asked Deborah thoughtfully as she sipped her tea.

"I don't rightly know, but I feels that Dazzle is beginning to believe he has been taken for a very expensive ride."

"Where does he send his paintings – to her gallery?"

"No. He sends them to a P.O. box number in London."

"London's a big place," stated Deborah. "Can you narrow it down?"

Yorrie trawled his memory for a few moments. "I think it's Chelsea. Is that a fashionable area do you know?"

"It certainly is, and full of art galleries and posey shops now. Look, I really don't think I should know about Dazzle's problems in this much detail," Deborah said, shifting in her chair.

"Oh please, help me sort this out for him. I'll go crackers living with him like this if we don't."

Deborah sighed. "OK. But if he finds out that we meddled, it was all your idea, remember?"

"Yes, yes, tidy I'll tell him it was all my idea."

Deborah sat forward, suddenly all business. "Right, this is the order in which we should tackle this imbroglio."

"Imbroglio?" queried Yorrie.

"Yes, it's a confusing, complicated problem. An imbroglio," explained Deborah.

Yorrie marvelled at her vocabulary. It showed the difference between a grammar and a comprehensive, he mused.

"First, we need to identify all the small art galleries in Chelsea associated with the name Susan Cartwright. I still know a couple of people I could contact who may be able to narrow things down for us." Deborah paused and smiled. "It's just like old times in the police when we were looking for a needle in a haystack."

Yorrie smiled back, delighted to be doing something constructive to help his friend and landlord.

"Next, perhaps you could check the franking on the envelopes on her letters, if Dazzle still has them. That may give us another clue as to where she might live. Then, if you could get hold of one of the envelopes, we might be able to extract some DNA from her licking the stamp. She may have form."

"Wow, you really are good, Deborah! I never would have thought of that in a million years!" Yorrie was genuinely impressed.

"Elementary, my dear Yorrie, elementary," said Deborah, clearly revelling in her audience's praise.

"We could even go to Chelsea together to find the P.O. box, and I could show you some of my old haunts," suggested Deborah coyly.

"I've never been to London and don't think I'd like it much." Yorrie ate one more Welsh cake, completely missing the innuendo.

Deborah shook her head in amazement. "I can't believe that there's anyone left in the 1990s who hasn't been to London." She started to describe the city, "Yorrie, London buzzes and hums for twenty-four hours a day. Sometimes it all speeds up and sometimes it all slows down, but it never stops. It's a city of endless layers where history and modernity intertwine horizontally and vertically. It's a strangely friendly city of Pearly Kings and Queens, of street artists and people watchers mixing with folk from a hundred different nations. You really would love it."

Yorrie listened to Deborah recounting her memories of London with a mix of memories and delight to be well away from its seedier side.

Deborah demonstrated the skyline with her hands. "Tower bridge arches right over the river Thames, watching the river traffic below. She has the ability to open and close the road sections to allow the tall ships through." She demonstrated the action with her fingers. She was in full swing. "The Tower of London was built by William the Conqueror, and still stands guard over London, murmuring tales of justice and injustice to visitors from all around the globe."

Deborah held her hand to her mouth and whispered, adding more theatre to her description, "The Tower can tell tales of horrors from centuries gone by and is gatekeeper to many more secrets still untold."

The descriptives were lost on Yorrie, who wasn't wholly convinced. He sipped at his tea thoughtfully, missing the mountains, the fields and the streams around his home, and the simple order of things that everyone understood.

Deborah poured herself more tea, added milk, and stirred enthusiastically. She continued, "The City is not just about history, it's also a vibrant collection of skyscrapers securing London's position on the whole world's stage of finance and commerce. And I'm positive you would want to watch the Covent Garden Street performers for hours on end. The London markets will push Swansea market into a cocked hat. We just have to go one day, Yorrie, we really must."

"I'll think about it," replied Yorrie, with no conviction at all.

"Anyway, back to the matter-in-hand," said Deborah with authority. "I'll see if I can get some old pals to help. You check out the letter franking and try to borrow one of the envelopes. Let's meet up again on Friday."

"Thanks, Deborah. You're being such a help, you really are," said Yorrie.

———

Friday couldn't come soon enough for Yorrie, for Dazzle was deep in self-wallowing mode and hardly communicating with him at all, or anyone else for that matter. Susan, or more accurately her absence, was beginning to affect his art.

Deborah poured coffee for Yorrie, complete with his two heaped spoons of sugar and asked him, "Why doesn't Dazzle go to London himself?"

"He hates confrontation of any sort. He's an artist in every sense of the word. He would sooner lose the money than have any sort of battle over it," replied Yorrie, taking his drink and settling into one of her deep sofas.

"Well, how did you get on with the envelopes?" she asked excitedly.

Yorrie explained the difficulties he had experienced, "I had to get him thoroughly pissed to get a look at them. There are two different franking stamps – one from Islington and the other from Westminster, I think. It's a bit smudged."

Deborah raised her eyebrows. "Westminster is interesting."

"Why?" asked Yorrie.

"One of my old colleagues, Billy Laptop, who is quite senior in art theft recovery–"

"Billy Laptop?" interrupted Yorrie. "Who the hell is Billy Laptop?" He laughed.

"He was called Billy Laptop because he was a particularly small constable at one of my stations. Mind you, he had a knack of finding villains who eluded everyone else. Satisfied?"

Yorrie rolled his eyes skyward. "A small PC? Laptop? That's weird."

"Anyway," continued Deborah, "When I spoke to him, Billy said there was an S. J. Cartwright who owned an art gallery in Chelsea, but her registered home address was in Westminster."

"That's great, isn't it? Isn't it?" queried Yorrie.

Deborah grimaced. "Well, no, because the art gallery has been shut for three years."

A long silence filled the room.

"What does that mean then?" Yorrie poured himself some more coffee and added sugar while Deborah thought.

"Not sure. There are a dozen explanations and to jump to any conclusions at this stage or tell Dazzle anything might lead to him making all sorts of accusations that might not be true, and any possible relationship between him and Susan will be flushed down the toilet. How did you get on with the stamp?"

"I had to lie through my teeth to get it," said Yorrie, proudly. "I told him he'd spilled a pint of mild all over it when he was pissed. I said he had soaked it so badly I chucked it away and put the letter into a clean envelope. So here you are – envelope and stamp." Yorrie retrieved them from his pocket and passed them to Deborah triumphantly.

"Remind me never to play poker with you," said Deborah wryly as she examined the letter and stamp.

8

Dazzle's mood was getting lower and lower as the excuses continued to arrive from Susan. He found himself debating the real reason behind the rejection, as he saw it. He decided it was perfectly natural to feel as he did when the trust in the relationship had been so eroded.

He asked himself if this was the beginning of the end? He asked himself if he was doing something wrong, and if her excuses not to meet up were his fault? Dazzle considered trying to talk to Yorrie, but knew full well there would be a saying from his old dad.

It would probably be something like, "Well my old dad used to say when a relationship of mine was going as pear-shaped as yours: 'Don't fret m' lad. As one door closes another one slams shut!'" Or his tenant might say, "I think you were too good for her anyway!" Or, "Love is a journey not a destination." As Yorrie wasn't that sensitive, Dazzle parked that idea.

He wondered if Susan had the foggiest idea how upset he was at the situation? Didn't she understand how much he cared for her? His mind was an emotional washing machine.

All the clues indicated that sadly this wasn't the solid relationship he thought they had been starting. Things appeared to be different now – more one sided. Mandy flitted back into his mind occasionally and he compared her pixie smile to Susan's more serious demeanour.

However, maybe, just maybe, he was reading far too much into her letters? Perhaps he was being just too sensitive? Perhaps she was as disappointed as he was that she couldn't get to see him? Perhaps he had driven her away with his letter about what money she owed? Could it be that in London everyone took a much more casual attitude towards relationships when they were apart?

Together, they had laughed about school episodes, but when thoughtful conversations needed to be aired, she could be very serious. She was everything he needed in a woman, which made his analysis of the situation even more poignant.

The circumstances were consuming all his waking thoughts. He didn't know how to manage all these feelings and uncertainties. Even worse, his painting was now suffering.

9

Yorrie couldn't wait to hear the postage stamp DNA results from Deborah.

"There's some good news and some bad news," said Deborah as she passed the butter for Yorrie to spread on his Bara Brith.

"Go on."

She continued, "I contacted my old friend Bobby Sandwich, and he said–"

Yorrie jumped in. "Bobby Sandwich? That's never his real name! Who the hell is Bobby Sandwich?"

"He was just a rookie copper when he worked for me," said Deborah.

"Did he like sandwiches in general or did he have favourites like beef and pickle or cheese and ham?" joked Yorrie.

"For goodness' sake, Yorrie, it was his nickname, and it had nothing to do with catering," explained Deborah with a note of irritation in her voice.

"Well, why could anyone get called Bobby Sandwich if it had nothing to do with sandwiches?"

Deborah sighed. "If you must know, it had something to do with two women. Satisfied?"

Yorrie thought for a moment then roared with laughter. "Bobby Sandwich! That's very good. Did everyone have a nickname then?"

"Yes," snapped Deborah, clearly losing patience.

"What was yours?"

"Oh, I can't remember. Can we get on?"

"Please try."

"OK, if you must know, it was Fang."

"Fang? Why Fang?" queried a nervous Yorrie, now regretting interjecting and not really wanting to hear the explanation.

Slightly raising her voice, Deborah said, "Because when things weren't going well for us, I had a reputation for biting folks heads off. OK, now can we get on?"

Yorrie nodded. He logged the name and decided he'd tread carefully around Fang, but replied, "Well, I think you're a pussy cat now." He gave her a hug.

"Thank you." Deborah snatched a Welsh cake from the plate and continued, "Anyway, Bobby said the saliva was not from Susan J. Cartwright at all. It was from a man. A man called Giacomo Hustletti. The only way Bobby could give him a name is because he has form. He's been inside for – wait for it – art theft! He also goes by the nickname 'Giacomo Trickasso' amongst his dodgy contemporaries in 'art redistribution' circles."

"Wasn't Giacomo the first name of a famous lover in Italy?" Yorrie racked his brains then blurted out, "Casanova! Yes, it was Giacomo Casanova. He had lots of sayings attributed to him. Didn't he say, 'Love is three quarters curiosity.' Or was that my old dad?" he mused.

"Thank you, Yorrie," Deborah patiently replied, rolling her eyes. "You are right, but that Giacomo was a famous author, lover and courtier. Not someone who nicked famous paintings and flogged them on."

"No link then?"

"No. Giacomo Hustletti is more of a middleman, like a fence is for burglars. Another link is that Giacomo seems to sell stolen paintings from Britain into the international marketplace. He appears to have many contacts in – wait for it – Italy."

Yorrie's eyes lit up. "I think I can remember Dazzle saying Susan liked spending time in Italy."

"It's all beginning to fit," said Deborah thoughtfully.

"What does all this mean then?" Yorrie took up the thread from there. "I assume Giacomo Hustletti licked the stamp because Susan asked him to posts a letter for her and she didn't have a stamp. He could be her lover, or someone who works for her and just happens to be an art thief. Doesn't look good for Dazzle, though, does it? Whichever way you look at it," said Yorrie as he fingered his now cold cup of tea.

"No, it doesn't," agreed Deborah, grimly shaking her head.

"What should we do next then? Tell the police?"

"Certainly not," snapped Deborah. "We don't want the plod tramping all over this in their size ten boots. We need to link all this together and have the full story before we involve them."

"I thought you worked for the police," asked a perplexed Yorrie.

"I did and that's exactly why I don't want them involved, not just yet. We don't have enough evidence." Deborah began pacing around her spacious lounge in thinking mode. Yorrie could imagine her doing exactly the same thing in uniform in her office when she was a Chief Superintendent.

"Right, this is what I think we should do..." She spoke with such authority and Yorrie remembered her nickname was Fang. "We should have someone on the ground for us in London. Not the police, someone private."

"Whoa!" Yorrie said. "Not so fast. Won't hiring a private dick or private eye cost an arm and a leg, especially in London?"

"You watch too much TV," replied Deborah.

"Aren't they all regulated by some government body or other in the UK?" asked Yorrie, trying to slow things down to his pedestrian brain speed.

"UK art investigators who are only looking at provenance and history do not need to be regulated. They only need to be regulated by the Security Industry Authority if they engage in surveillance of individuals."

Yorrie frowned. "But aren't we hoping these investigators will check up on individuals like Susan or Giacomo?"

"Not initially. We will be looking for the history of the art gallery and where the paintings, sent by Dazzle, have gone."

"As my old dad would ask, 'Is your name Icarus?'"

"Icarus?" queried Deborah, giving him a blank look.

"It means are you flying too close to the sun? We still mustn't let Dazzle know anything about this just in case it is all above board and there is a happy ending. I'd never forgive myself if I buggered it up for him."

"OK, I'll just talk to a few people, if you prefer, and get some advice. I'll stay in generalities mode and not use Dazzle's name or yours at all. I promise. Is that better?"

"Thanks, Deborah. Plus, if he finds out anything about this, I'll be homeless within the hour."

"There will always be a place for you here," said Deborah coyly. Yorrie smiled at her.

10

Dazzle was beginning to draw attention to himself. He was becoming withdrawn, and his art was beginning to suffer. Miss Bumfuzzled, was brave enough to speak to him about it. She cornered him one bright winter's day and asked outright, "What's the matter, Daz?"

"Nothing really, just relationship problems," he replied.

She caught hold of his arm and took him out of earshot of any other customers and whispered in his ear, "Never mind, dearie. I'm always here. Just give me a little time to get ready, if you know what I mean." She winked at him.

Dazzle looked at her in shock for a moment then the two of them fell about laughing.

"That's better," she said. "Much more like my old Dazzle. I thought it would make you smile." With that, she left but not before she had looked back, given him another wink and showed him a flash of her ankle.

Mr. Papadopoulos also offered him some words of wisdom. "Stay yourself single, Dazzle. I have had three wives. Now I poor and have just Bruno. He best companion of all wives. After wife number three my son, he say, 'Dad, you deserve medal as big as dustbin lid.' I laugh, he laugh, and we got drunk together. Maybe you should try it. I happy to get drunk with you one day."

Dazzle said he would think about it. He was currently only selling one or two paintings a week and still sending two a month to Susan in London. He checked the post every day to see if there had been a reply to his request for some money. There had been no correspondence from her this week, and she was due to arrive on Friday evening.

Dazzle was hanging on to hope by a thinner and thinner thread and getting more nervous by the day; it was five months since he had seen her. He was desperate to see her, which made him snap at Yorrie for the smallest thing. He knew he wasn't being fair, but he was living on tenterhooks.

———

On Wednesday – the day Susan usually wrote to cancel – Yorrie went over to Deborah's, pleased to get away from Dazzle.

Upon opening the door, her words were, "We need to have a conversation."

Yorrie was struck by the formality. He felt he was being summoned by a headmistress.

"We do?" asked Yorrie wondering what he had done wrong – had he offended her or upset her wanting to know what her nickname was?

"Yes, we do. Back home in North Wales, you went to the

local comprehensive school, and I went to the county grammar school, right?" fired Deborah at him.

"Right?" Yorrie felt like a rabbit in the headlights. He had no idea where the conversation was leading.

"So, we're of a similar age," stated Deborah.

"Give or take a year or two. I think you are a touch older than me but hey-ho it doesn't show... much," said Yorrie, trying to lighten the mood. Deborah ignored the slight and Yorrie realised this was serious.

"And you went to chapel regular as clockwork?" she asked.

"Every Sunday. Twice sometimes."

"And you were in the choir?"

"Aha, now you have me there. I was in the choir, until they asked me to sing on my own, that is. Up until then I had been miming just to make my mam proud. Once they heard me sing on my own, it was suggested I could contribute to the chapel in another way. I was put to work with the gardener."

"Well, apart from the choir, were we both God fearing Welsh children from God fearing Welsh families?" Deborah challenged.

"Yes," he replied nervously, expecting this to be the end of the only close relationship he had experienced in years.

"So why the hell haven't you kissed me yet?" demanded Deborah.

Yorrie gaped at her. "Because you were a Chief Superintendent in the bloody police force and I'm just a lowly cartographer. Our worlds are miles apart."

"I'll show you how far apart our worlds are," said Deborah, striding across the lounge towards him.

Yorrie stood up, terrified of what was going to happen next. Then Deborah kissed him, full on. Not a peck on the cheek but a full-blown French kiss. Yorrie was not ready for this and started to pull away but relaxed into the embrace and kissed her back.

"There, how was that then?" she asked when the clinch ended.

Yorrie's eyes were still rolling around in his head and he slumped down heavily onto the wheezing settee.

"Now we have that out of the way, let me tell you what I've found out. I've been in touch with another old friend. He suggests we make contact with a private investigating company calling itself A.B. Chevron. They are new on the scene in London and are making a name for themselves. They've been on several high-profile art theft cases already, and came up trumps each time. What do you think?"

"I think we should kiss again," said Yorrie dreamily.

"Yorrie, come down to earth and answer the question. We can do that again later."

"OK, OK, OK. Right, despite the fact that I am having trouble concentrating I agree we should talk to A.B. Chevron," said Yorrie. "However, I don't want my name involved at all so perhaps you could talk to them alone? By the way, how are we going to pay them?"

"We won't. I will."

"That's not fair, you shouldn't have to pay anything," replied Yorrie.

"It will be fine. I'll try and make the costs dependant on the results. There may be some rewards somewhere. I'll get them to do a few things: confirm the identified gallery in Chelsea is associated with Susan Cartwright, find out what's happened to the gallery and where all the stock is, find out where Susan Cartwright lives in Westminster, and then find out how Giacomo fit into all this. Oh, and find out where Dazzle's paintings are, or his money is.

Yorrie nodded in admiration. "Cracking, I can't thank you enough for helping. Not sure I would have known where to start without you," he admitted, and meant it.

"That's done with all the business. Now where were we?" said Deborah, walking purposefully across the lounge towards him again.

11

The end of February arrived and Dazzle watched and waited as the postman chatted idly to every person in the street, working his way slowly towards him. Eventually, he handed over a bundle of junk mail.

Dazzle quickly waded through the rubbish, threw it in the bin and breathed again. Good news: there was no letter from Susan cancelling their weekend.

On Thursday, again, there was no letter from Susan. Dazzle was over the moon. This meant she was coming. It also meant a tidy of the house was required, as well as a haircut and plenty of wine for two nights if they stayed in.

He scurried around, clearing everything that was in the wrong place. It was Yorrie who reminded him there were two deliveries of post some days. His heart sunk.

"What time does the second one normally come?" Dazzle demanded.

"No idea," replied Yorrie. "Nobody ever writes to me, not even on my birthday."

But by 6 p.m., there was no more post, and crucially, no letter from Susan saying she wasn't coming.

On Friday, Dazzle couldn't sit still. He jumped out of his chair every time a car drew up nearby. At 7.00 p.m. there was no Susan. At 8.00 p.m. there was no Susan. At 9.00 p.m. there was still no Susan. Nor at 10.00 p.m.

Dazzle unscrewed the cap off one of the wines and drank straight from the bottle. Some red wine ran down his cheeks and onto his jumper.

He offered the bottle to Yorrie who went into the kitchen and brought two wine glasses into the lounge. He poured two sensible measures and sat down opposite his landlord. They both knew tonight was going to get messy.

The night did get very messy. Five bottles of red wine were drunk between the two of them. One of them was a very modest drinker who became tiddly on wine gums and soon dropped out of the evening, and the other was a Welsh drinking Olympiad.

Yorrie helped Dazzle up to his bed and set him up with towels and a metal wastepaper bin by the side of his bed, just in case.

———

At 10 a.m. on Saturday morning Yorrie woke to the front door being hammered upon. He made his way downstairs in his boxers. Last time he opened the door to someone hammering it didn't end well. So, it was with caution he peeped out from behind the curtain.

"Oh God, no!" was all he could say. It was Susan, and she did not seem to be in a good mood. He opened the door slowly.

"Morning, Yorrie." She squeezed past him. "Or should I say afternoon?"

Yorrie wasn't sure what to say so suggested she was welcome to make herself a cup of tea.

"Where is he then?" demanded Susan.

"In bed."

"Poorly?"

Yorrie nodded.

"Today he will be," said Susan as she surveyed the five empty wine bottles. "I've driven all the way from London and when I arrive, he's hungover?"

"'Fraid so," admitted Yorrie. "I'll go and get him up."

Upstairs, the smell in Dazzle's room was appalling. Yorrie shook him till he woke. Or roused him from unconsciousness would be more accurate.

"Susan's here," he shouted.

Dazzle's eyes opened wide. Yorrie thought he looked like a lamb to the slaughter with eyes that were looking out but weren't seeing.

Ten minutes later Dazzle joined Yorrie and Susan downstairs. He was met with a very frosty welcome. Yorrie escaped to the adjoining kitchen, a prime spot for eavesdropping.

"My God, Dazzle, you look ghastly! And smell even worse."

"You didn't come yesterday," said Dazzle limply.

Susan's volume rose sharply, "I didn't come yesterday because my bloody car wouldn't start, and when I did get it fixed, I had a puncture halfway here. I got to the hotel after midnight. I didn't think you would want me to wake you then, so I went to bed. And all the while I was waiting for a breakdown lorry in the dark and the rain on the A23, you were getting pissed. I'll come back at 6.00 p.m. tonight, so be ready."

She stalked out, slamming the front door shut loudly.

Yorrie decided that contrary to her being a lovely, caring, ex-art teacher, she had just demonstrated she could well turn out to be 'the canary that killed the cat', as his old dad used to say. But he opted to keep his observations to himself.

Yorrie crept back into the lounge. Having been where Dazzle was many times before, he had become an expert on hangover recoveries.

"Right, we've got eight hours to get you firing on all cylinders, boyo. Let's start with rehydration. We need some electrolyte-replenishing beverages into you, like coconut water. It will rehydrate you. I'll go out and gets some. I'll also gets some ginger tea to soothe your stomach and some bananas, which are high in potassium. Before I go shopping though, I'll make some toast to settle your rumbling tum, which I can hear from here. It'll raise your blood sugars. How do you like your eggs?" he asked.

"I couldn't eat a thing," mumbled Dazzle.

"Oh, yes you bloody well can. And in the absence of a coherent answer, let's call it poached then. Eggs are rich in cysteine which helps to break down acetaldehyde, a toxic by-product of alcohol. You're having a couple of eggs, maybe three, maybe four. I'll also get some vitamin B and C supplements to restore your nutrient levels. So, get your arse off the sofa and go and have a shower, and the toast and eggs will be ready when you come down." He wagged his finger in Dazzle's face. "I'll be back with a bag of stuff for you before you've finished breakfast. Don't drink too much coffee as it'll just dehydrate you and reverse all the good I'm doing. After that, you must go to bed for at least six hours, as rest allows your body to recover through sleep. It's the best remedy there is. Trust me, I know about these things."

A grunt was all that was forthcoming from Dazzle.

"When you get up again," continued Yorrie, "I'll have some chicken broth ready to provide some more electrolytes and you'll finish off with some peppermint tea to help with the headaches and any digestive discomfort. A shave and another shower and you will be ready to take on Miss Grumpy Susan. OK? Oh, and don't forget what my old dad used to say: 'Being in love is like playing cards. First you play the hearts, then you play the diamonds and then the clubs. Finally, the spades.' I think you are in the clubs section just now, Daz."

Yorrie's dad's saying clearly hadn't registered with Dazzle. Without speaking, he rose unsteadily and headed upstairs.

———

On the dot of 6.00 p.m., there was the expected knock at the door. Dazzle opened it and Susan stepped inside.

"Ready for dinner?" she asked, seemingly calmer than earlier.

"Certainly," replied a transformed Dazzle. "Look, before we go out, please let me apologise for last night. I was so disappointed when I thought you weren't coming again."

"Shh, we've all been there. It's in the past." She smiled at him. "Before I forget, I didn't pick up my cheque book before I left, so I'm sorry too. We'll just have to sort the numbers out at a later date. I hope you aren't cross."

"Certainly not," replied Dazzle, just pleased she hadn't already left to go back to London.

12

_____

"What happened then?" asked Deborah, intrigued, as she put some Garibaldis out for Yorrie on Sunday afternoon.

"How should I know? I didn't follow them to the hotel or out for dinner," he said, taking a couple of biscuits.

"Convenient she forgot her cheque book," suggested Deborah sarcastically. "I thought she gave him a bundle of cash the previous times."

Yorrie swallowed. "You're right! When she first came, she always brought him cash. I didn't register that. Next time I'll see them will be tonight when she'll drop him off and collect two more of his paintings. Then he'll sleep till Tuesday, maybe Wednesday, and with a bit of luck, he'll be in a better mood by then, unless he's been unable to hang it all together then he will be like death."

Yorrie shook his head at the thought. Wanting to change the subject, he coyly ventured his intentions, "How about we forget about Dazzle and Susan for a while, put some soft music on, and you come and join me here on the sofa?" Yorrie patted the cushion next to him.

"In a while, OK?" Deborah said as she poured tea for the two of them. Yorrie did his best to disguise his sigh of disappointment as Deborah continued talking about Susan. "Her coming here hasn't filled me with any confidence that Dazzle's problems are over. In fact, it's made me think we're probably dealing with a very cunning vixen. I think her next step will be to absent herself from the next two planned weekends, then come for another short stay minus her cheque book. Then disappear for ever. I wonder if she is doing the same thing to half a dozen other artists," she pondered.

"On the other hand," said Yorrie, trying his best to be positive, "she is here now and the reasons for her absences over the last few months and her lateness last night are all plausible. We need to keep an open mind and be sure Dazzle never hears a word about our investigations."

"Our investigations – oh yes, I nearly forgot." Deborah took a breath. "My people, sorry, my old friend Snoz – and before you ask, I have no idea why he was called Snoz and neither has anyone else – who used to work in recovering illicitly obtained art, said this form of thieving was very lucrative and surrounded in opacity. Snoz was a bloody good and very experienced copper, so everyone listened to him. He told me that many cities in Europe have reputations for dealing in looted or stolen art. Paris, for example, with its rich colonial heritage has been a centre for a century. Antwerp trades in diamonds, and Italy trades in looted artifacts from Rome and Greece. Madrid focusses on modern art works. Are you following?" she checked.

Yorrie nodded dutifully.

"So, Snoz suggested that some of these centres are part of a broader global market place intertwined with organised crime and money laundering. He warned me these villains are not to be trifled with for the rewards are immense and they will kill on sight, but I knew that. He's given me the name and contact details of that new company I told you about – A.B. Chevron. The one that seems to be making a name for itself in the art theft investigation world already?"

Yorrie nodded again, nibbling on another biscuit.

"Well, I called and spoke to a woman called Bernadette Westerman who explained they undertook work in due diligence, corporate investigations, fraud investigations and surveillance. I explained what I wanted, and she listened to me without interrupting, and when I had finished, she asked sensible, clarifying questions. She appeared to be quite sharp and professional, and I am a mean judge of character from years of working with villains. So, I commissioned the company, there and then, to make the enquiries we discussed. She said someone would come back to me in a few days."

Yorrie continued to listen, his pedestrian mind whirring at the speed things were happening.

"Well, she rang me back this morning with a quick update. One of their investigators was working in Chelsea and he called around to all the galleries within a half a mile of the centre. They found that one gallery had been closed for about three years. The floor space appears to be completely empty. Some of locals said nobody ever goes there. A.B. Chevron then did a desk search on that gallery. It was registered to Miss S. J. Cartwright and a Mr. Giacomo Hustletti, who paid business rates on it until a couple of years ago. It's on the property market at the moment. A.B. Chevron are now working on getting current addresses for the two ex-owners."

"Wow, that was quick!" exclaimed Yorrie, eyes open wide. "I'm impressed, aren't you?"

"Yes, Bernadette appears to be very efficient. Let's see how they get on with the next bit." She stood up. "Time to go out for a walk along the promenade while the weather holds out, to clear our heads."

Yorrie sighed as he looked out of the window at the last leaves blowing off the trees in the March winds.

"If we must."

————

The day after Susan went home was strange for Dazzle. He wasn't sure if he'd been forgiven or not. He felt the slightest level of tension had been wedged between them. Nothing he could put his finger upon but, being easily hurt, he could sense it. Nothing was said, but the faintest chill had entered their relationship.

He immediately blamed himself and put it down to his behaviour on Friday evening. Susan had every right to be cross; she had driven from London, and he had let himself down. If they did lose touch, he believed it would be due to his own stupidity. Fancy getting pissed because she was late – how childish was that? And this time he couldn't blame Yorrie. In fact, Yorrie saved the day for him with his electrolytes and chicken broth. Had he been on his own, Dazzle would have dragged himself through the day and still looked a real mess when she returned. As it was, after his tenant's sleep and potions, he felt OK, and was able to keep going for the evening and all the next day. He decided he would put his hangover to bed during the rest of the week, and never make the same mistake again.

13

One evening, Dazzle and Yorrie were having a discussion in the lounge. It wasn't going Yorrie's way.

"But wouldn't it be a better idea than putting up all that ripped polythene every wet Sunday to protect your amazing work? It really doesn't look professional at all, does it? Be honest, Daz. All we needs to do is find a suitable building on the promenade and invite the artists to chip in to pay the rent. If it's a local authority building, you may well not have to pay any rent at all. If it's a genuine social enterprise, we could offer coffee and teacakes at a reasonable price to keep the customers happy and keep the costs down. Bob's your uncle!"

Dazzle could hardly contain his laughter at Yorrie's idea, and Yorrie was embarrassed by Dazzle's reaction to what he believed would be a really great move forward for the local artists.

"You make it sound so simple, but it would be like pushing water uphill," a genuinely disillusioned Dazzle replied. "Never in a million years," he added.

A strong rebuke was forthcoming from Yorrie, who spoke very slowly and quietly, "Nothing ever happened on this globe for good, at which some people did not have their fill of laughter at the outset."

"Is that another of your dad's sayings?" asked Dazzle after mulling over the comment.

"No, Charles Dickens."

Dazzle shook his head. "The artists just wouldn't buy into your idea."

"Of course they would. It's a cracking idea, if you sold it properly," insisted Yorrie.

"I know them. They might feign interest at the start but getting them to change the way they have always done things would be almost impossible. And like me, I'm sure they don't have any spare cash."

"I'm happy with 'almost impossible'. I can work with 'almost impossible'," argued Yorrie enthusiastically. "I'm absolutely convinced it could work and I'm sure they would come around as the idea gathered some momentum. In fact, if truth be told it's the best idea I've ever had."

"I'm really not sure," replied Dazzle.

Yorrie ignored the onslaught of barriers being erected in front of his idea. "You could staff it with people who are available on a rota basis, and it would soon become the 'hub on the prom' which folk want to come to. Success would breed success. And don't forget there would be nothing stopping you painting in your section of the gallery, with better light than here, while you waited for customers. That's something you can't do on the promenade in the wind and rain, can you?"

"Hmm, you have a point there, Yorrie," said Dazzle, finally pondering the suggestion as he brushed the remains of his Welsh cake into his hand and emptied them into his mouth, not wanting to waste a crumb.

"You could also sell every day of the week, not just Sundays, and no matter the weather, right through the year."

Yorrie could sense Dazzle's change in mood so decided to push a little harder. "I chatted this idea over with Deborah, and she said she'd heard on the grapevine that the old Baptist church on the front is to be closed in two months' time. It's in a prime position and has a large seating area outside facing the sea. You'll have to move like lightning before it goes on the market, or it will be snapped up and turned into another dreadful fast food restaurant, rock shop or slot machine parlour, all of which we have a surfeit. Your gallery could become St Cuthbert Bay's oasis of culture."

"Have you or Deborah ever been involved with a social enterprise like this before?" asked Dazzle

Yorrie nodded. "We've both been involved in different ways. Me when I was between jobs, or 'resting' as they say in theatrical circles, and Deborah set one up from scratch."

"How did you go about it then? How did you get started?"

Yorrie leaned forward. "She believes the very first thing is to find a local investor who wants to make a social impact in the town. Someone who could help us influence the council, and access grants, subsidies or low interest loans. Their role would be vital. She believes she already knows a few she could approach. She is one formidable person when she sets her mind on something. Trust me, I know," said Yorrie.

"Go on," encouraged Dazzle.

"Well, from where I stands, customers appear to value ethical and sustainable ventures like this one. They gets a buzz from encouraging and supporting up-and-coming artists like you. Just as well 'cos otherwise we'd be eating veggie casserole for breakfast, dinner and supper."

"Mmm," mumbled Dazzle.

"You could persuade the papers to do a splash on the gallery by tackling important local problems like unemployment and homelessness. Looking after myself, I am." Yorrie chuckled. "During the school holidays, perhaps, you could run some painting classes for children. Thinking out of the box, I am. Young holidaymakers could be attracted to enterprises that align with their values and your gallery would be spot on for the old folk and their grey pounds. And as the gallery gains momentum, you could attract artists from all over the south coast. This could be big, Daz, real big."

Dazzle smiled as Yorrie concluded his animated speech. "Are you on something?" he asked.

"Yes, I'm on passion, purpose, and growing something amazing! That's what I'm on. And, because the gallery would be run by artists for artists, we'd have no wages costs, no H.R., and no contracts of employment, and the like. The gallery would have the dual purpose of profit and purpose. It could become the model for the south coast. What do you think?"

"I'm in," said Dazzle, nodding enthusiastically. "I'd need to get all the local artists together on the Q. T. to see if there is a real appetite for the idea first. However, if there isn't enough support, then I'm out, OK?"

"OK," agreed Yorrie. "But they would need to be bonkers not to see all the benefits!"

Dazzle smiled widely. "Thanks, Yorrie."

Excitedly, Yorrie left to tell Deborah how the meeting with Dazzle had gone.

"He's in! Daz is in!" shouted Yorrie as soon as Deborah opened the front door.

14

The phone rang in Deborah's lounge. Following the usual business pleasantries, the A. B. Chevron secretary put Bernadette through to Deborah. She explained that Miss S. J. Cartwright and a Mr. Giacomo Hustletti lived at the same address in Westminster – an up-market premises which Miss Cartwright had solely owned for ten years.

Bernadette added that Miss Cartwright had been a teacher of art in a senior school, had been married with no children for ten years when her marriage broke down, and that she and her husband subsequently divorced. It was not acrimonious, and she had been given a large sum of money by her ex-husband, as a once-and-for-all settlement, which allowed her to purchase the address in Westminster and the gallery in Chelsea.

Deborah listened to the flow of information, then asked, "Was her gallery business profitable?"

"Yes, according to our sources, her gallery was very profitable," confirmed Bernadette. "When she ran a promotional event, tickets were changing hands at ten times their face value. She sold a mix of well-established and up-and-coming artists' work from all over the country."

"How did she acquire her stock of paintings for sale?" asked Deborah.

"Mmm, this is the interesting bit," said Bernadette. "Miss Cartwright employs a number of part-time 'finders'. The Modus Operandi is simple: these finders travel around town and village art shows in the UK, seeking out talented artists. When they find an outstanding painter, they offer to display their work in a popular London art gallery. The offer is beyond the wildest dreams of the artist and far too lucrative to turn down. Once seduced by the finders, the unsuspecting artists are hooked and start producing for the London gallery. Apart from the initial payments for say one or two paintings, the money soon dries up and the unsuspecting artists continue painting on the promise of money in the future. Very few artists have the wherewithal to pursue the finders, and so the artists just write the experience off after about six to nine months."

"Susan Cartwright and Giacomo Hustletti really are bastards," snapped Deborah.

Bernadette agreed and continued, "Local Chelsea knowledge suggests the gallery was very popular during the week, benefitting from a substantial footfall. Miss Cartwright also ran very fashionable weekend exhibitions. It was at one of these champagne promotions for her artists we believe she met Mr. Hustletti."

"Is the name Hustletti Italian?" asked Deborah.

"Yes, however, Mr. Hustletti was considerably more elusive. The first record of his criminal existence, as far as we can establish, was a short stay at Her Majesty's Pleasure for being involved in a large art theft in Italy. However, his role in the theft was small. He brought some of the stolen paintings to England to dispose of them. He came out of prison about three years ago on parole and has kept his head down ever since. He exists under the radar with no driving licence, no job, no income and no National Insurance number. We can confirm, however, that after surveilling him, he spends virtually all his life squirrelled away in the house he shares in Westminster. That is, apart from some local shopping and the occasional trip to a betting shop down the road where he makes modest bets on horses. Hot food is regularly delivered to the property, and if Mr. Hustletti answers the door, he pays with Miss Cartwright's credit card. He never tips according to the local Indian restaurant manager, but she does. I'm sorry, but that is all we have been able to find out about him so far."

"Thank you, Bernadette. Based on your experience, do you believe this is all there is to Miss Cartwright?" probed Deborah.

"Definitely not! Based on the evidence collected so far, it's all a bit too neat, if you know what I mean, and Mr. Hustletti muddies the water."

"Thank you very much. I now need to go away, digest everything you've told me, and discuss it with my colleague. I do not believe this is the end of the matter and would like to contact A. B. Chevron again soon, to investigate further. Your first staged payment will be in the post today as promised. Good day and thank you." Deborah replaced the receiver thoughtfully.

————

That evening, Yorrie arrived at Deborah's home. The pleasantries were summarily dispensed with and he sat down, ready to hear all the news. Deborah was clearly in work mode and demanded not to be interrupted. She repeated her call from earlier in the day with Bernadette.

"Questions?" she demanded when she was done.

"Why, if she doesn't have a gallery, does she still employ people to look for new paintings?" asked Yorrie, reaching for a custard cream biscuit.

"Really good question, and I don't know the answer," said Deborah, hunching her shoulders as she walked around the room.

"Mind you, if she's not paying for them then there's no cost to her," added Yorrie, quickly moving on to the Welsh cakes.

"True. But where is she storing them? What will she do with them?" questioned Deborah, talking as much to herself as to Yorrie.

Yorrie took over, "I'll bet the artists don't know anything about her. All their dealings will have been with the finders, and I'll bet one pound to a piece of… something unpleasant that she keeps miles away from them so there's no audit trail."

"Probably." Deborah nodded in agreement. "You sure you didn't work for the Met at some time?" she asked, clearly impressed with his logical thinking.

"No, but as a cartographer I had to do masses of research into disputes over ancient rights of way. It makes you think differently, laterally, I suppose. Do you think the time has come when we should talk to Dazzle?" Yorrie tentatively suggested.

"No, definitely not! Apart from Geopedro, or whatever his bloody name is, we have nothing more than Dazzle already knows. He knows she has a gallery, lives in London, goes around collecting pictures to sell, and has a soft spot for him."

"Hmm, you're probably right. I just don't like withholding all the other stuff we knows." Yorrie shrugged.

"I think we should let A. B. Chevron do some more digging into who the finders are, how they get the paintings to Susan, and what she does with them. Can you remember the address Dazzle sends his paintings to?"

"P.O. Box 20779715, Jury Street, Chelsea," replied Yorrie, reciting the address from memory.

"Are you sure?" queried Deborah, opening a notebook and searching for a pen.

"Yes, it's easy. Just think of the numbers as grid squares on an ordinance survey map. In really simple terms, the first four digits are the Eastings and the second four are the Northings. Eastings are along the bottom of a map and the Northings are up the right-hand side of the map. Or as my old lecturer used to say, 'First you have to go along the hall before you go up the stairs to get to your ten-metre bed.'"

"If you say so. You never cease to amaze me." Deborah shook her head as she wrote down the numbers. "I'll pass it on to A. B. Chevron to follow up," she said.

15

While Yorrie and Deborah were enjoying a day out, Dazzle stayed at home, spiralling down in emotional turmoil because Susan had missed another weekend visit. Whenever he felt this way, he found solace in undertaking research into the watercolour masters through the ages. He always started with J. M. W. Turner who died in 1851, who had what is considered to be the most significant influence on art history. Turner was regarded as the master of light and atmosphere in watercolours. Dazzle painstakingly considered Turner's landscapes and seascapes, trying to understand how he was able to replicate the true beauty of nature. Dazzle felt he just wanted to walk into Turner's paintings and studied every brush stroke and flow of colour.

Try as he might, Dazzle had never been able to copy Turner's delicate washes of colour that stirred his emotions. His mind drifted back to something Susan said about his paintings at their first meeting the previous year.

She had said, 'Dazzle you interpret the changing play of light on water well. Mist, rain and the flow of water baffle even the most skilful of artists. Now you've lost the desire to try to paint images but now you are focussed on capturing the essence of a scene for the viewer to interpret.'

She'd been right. He was trying to emulate Turner's style of not trying to paint a series of images and superimposing them in order on a canvas, but presenting the whole scene for the viewer to make of it what they want.

Susan was good at explaining his style to him. She had been right about many things that evening, and during their subsequent meetings. She had an understanding about him. She wasn't trying to flatter him but position him on his artistic journey and encourage him to know where to concentrate next. Her vision came into his artist's mind and he could imagine every flick of her hair, every turn of her head, and her wry smile as she gave her interpretation of his work.

"Bloody woman!" he shouted across the lonely room. "Get out of my head! You're the reason I'm in this state. I need to get up and do something physical. I need tea and biscuits to clear you out of my mind." He jumped out of his chair and headed for the kitchen. Noisily, he banged the kettle on to the hob and lit the flame below it. He left it symbolically on fierce. When the kettle began boiling, he warmed the china teapot. Now more controlled, he carefully measured out two spoons full of loose tea. Cup and milk ready, he unscrewed the lid off the biscuit barrel and at the bottom there were… crumbs. Broken biscuit crumbs.

Dazzle tutted. "Bloody Yorrie! Why on earth did I expect anything else?" he asked the kitchen sink. He rummaged around, looking for something to eat. He gave up when Thursday's reheated vegetable casserole entered his head. When ready, he poured the tea and returned to his book of influential artists.

Dazzle flicked the page open at Edward Hopper, who died more recently than Turner. Hopper was a very accomplished watercolourist. What captured Dazzle's imagination was his focus on light and shadow. How the intensity of light and its direction altered the image, whether it was a hard light creating sharp shadows, or soft light creating blurred edges to images. With a magnifying glass he followed the source of light and the impact it had on each shadow in Hopper's paintings. Some shadows were elongated by both sunrise and sun set. He noted that all the shadows were carefully positioned on slightly different lines to the sun. Dazzle deduced that here was a master in the art of chiaroscuro, which meant using strong contrasts to give the wonderful illusion of three dimensions.

He was deep in thought about his next painting and how he could adopt some of these techniques to enhance his work. It would be a seascape from the beach of a tiny cove nearby.

In his mind's eye he envisioned the surf, the cliffs, the rocks and every shadow left by an interesting, rotting hulk of an old clinker-built rowing boat. It was a cove that he and Susan had visited several times. His memory drifted to swimming together close to the nearly deserted beach, of playful splashing like children. There had been good times. There really had. Tears welled up in his eyes. He felt he was losing something special and had no way of reversing it.

Angrily, he turned the pages to John Constable's art and there was Susan again, in his mind, staring back at him. Not sneering, not laughing, just there. He slammed the book shut and cleared everything away, hoping to clear her away too.

As he left the house, Yorrie was walking up the short path, back from his day out with Deborah.

"Fancy a walk?" asked Dazzle.

"Why not?" said Yorrie, turning on his heel. "Anywhere in particular?"

"No, just to get that bloody woman out of my head."

"Oh, that sort of a walk."

"Yes, I just can't get her out of everything I do," grumbled Dazzle.

"But everything you do has a connection to Susan," Yorrie reminded him. "You're painting into the early hours of the morning just to satisfy her demands for extra paintings. We are living hand to mouth because she hasn't paid you in months. I can see why she is commanding such a big piece of your life."

"You're right, but how do I get her out of my mind?"

They walked in silence for a while.

"Well, you could try mindfulness," suggested Yorrie. "When she comes into your head, you observe her without reacting. Or you could try deep breathing exercises."

"That's all a bit 'bean bag and joss stick brigade' for me," dismissed Dazzle. "I want something practical."

"How about limiting the triggers that bring her to mind in the house? How about a new hobby that fills your time with fresh experiences and new people? Or exercise? Physical activity has been shown to improve mental health and reduce stress."

Dazzle listened to his tenant, digesting his ideas.

"What about practising gratitude and self-compassion? Listing all the things you're grateful for or just being kind to yourself. What about getting away from here for a few days? It would be a tonic."

By this time, they had arrived at the pub they were thrown out of some months ago.

"Fancy a pint?" asked Yorrie.

Dazzle glanced at his tenant. "Yes, but remember, don't you go anywhere near the bar. Let me order this time," he insisted.

———

"Happy Birthday, Yorrie!" announced Deborah, speaking between puffs on a noisy party blower. She handed him a balloon.

"Uh?" asked Yorrie.

"April 20th – your birthday. It is, isn't it? questioned Deborah.

Yorrie thought for a moment and then said, "Do you know, you're right. But hows do you know?"

"Bobby," said Deborah.

"Bobby Sandwich?"

"The very one. I would have been gutted if I'd missed it by a few days, but as luck would have it, I found out a week ago."

"What else did he tell you about me?" queried Yorrie.

"Well, you're broke so you don't have to worry that I'm after your money. It must be something else." She winked at him.

He took the comment as a compliment. Laughing, he gave her a hug.

"I have a present for you too." She handed him a large envelope wrapped in bright birthday paper and ribbons.

Excitedly, he said, "I can't recollect the last time anyone remembered my birthday. Not even my family. Christmas cards, yes, but birthdays? Never. Thank you so much."

"You may not like it," she warned.

"I'm sure I will love it."

He ripped open the package as if he was ten years old. Deborah smiled as she watched him excitedly tearing the paper off.

"Wow, Lion King theatre tickets! I listen to all the songs. Where in St. Cuthbert's Bay is it on?"

"London," said Deborah.

"London?"

"Yep, the smoke!" She smiled widely at him.

"Fantastic. There are two tickets – are you coming too?" asked Yorrie naively.

"Yes, I'll come too."

"Good. I'm sure to get lost," he said.

"Even though you're a cartographer?" Deborah shook her head.

"Where are we staying?" asked Yorrie.

"In a modest London hotel," she confirmed.

"You're a star," he said, and he kissed her. Not a peck on the cheek but a real kiss for someone who had done something special... just for him.

16

In the absence of Susan, Dazzle put aside his initial reticence and arranged a meeting of all the artists he believed might take to the idea of a permanent gallery on the promenade. There were twenty-five in total. They were added to Deborah's influential friends and Yorrie made it up to thirty. The idea of hosting the event in his cramped house were quickly dispelled as the numbers added up. It was Yorrie who had the brainwave of actually hosting it in the Baptist church as it was still functioning as a place of worship.

A modest hire cost was agreed, and the meeting was scheduled for a Sunday night, after evening service. One of Deborah's friends, Richard Green, who also held the position of town councillor, agreed to chair the proceedings.

Richard opened the meeting by thanking Dazzle, Yorrie and Deborah for sharing the idea with them all. He went on to say that he had been involved in a couple of similar ventures and that they were all fraught with problems, albeit different problems, and there were no quick fixes. Working with church administrators could take decades as they were only used to working one day a week! The atmosphere was immediately lightened with laughter.

"Anyway, moving on, first of all, let me confirm we are all here for the same reason. Currently, artists can only sell to the public on a Sunday, on the promenade, come rain or shine. The new idea is to work together to acquire a building, divide it up into studios and sell your art seven days a week, come rain or shine. This lovely old chapel on the promenade is your first choice. Am I right?" he asked the group.

A positive sound came from the gathered artists.

"It's always a good start to know we are all here for the same reason and not for a choir practice. Now, on to some of the issues you will have to consider. You will need to decide if you want to lease, rent or buy the property. A third option is buying the property outright. For this approach one of you artists will have to produce a Turner quality painting or a Constable, sell it and buy the property outright, but as most painters are only recognised posthumously it's a high price for one of you to pay."

The audience warmed to Richard's humour, and Dazzle noticed nobody spoke whilst he was speaking.

Richard continued, "Disused chapels, while often cheaper than commercial properties, can still require a significant financial commitment. A group of artists may need a stable income to cover monthly rent, utilities, and upkeep. Securing grants, subsidies, or sponsorships could be avenues to pursue, but arts funding is highly competitive. That's where I come in. I write bids for grants and, on your behalf, I would bid for any other monies to contribute to the rent."

Dazzle looked over at Yorrie and smiled. His tenant's suggestion was starting to look like a real possibility.

Richard went on, "Older buildings often require more maintenance. Heating, plumbing, and electrical systems may need upgrading, and repairs can be costly, potentially overwhelming the group's budget. However, two of my colleagues here have had a very quick look around the chapel, and they say it seems to be in very good order for its age. That's a very big advantage to you."

Many of the gathered artists were nodding their heads, their expressions hopeful.

"We would also need to find out if the building is listed," said Richard. "Chapels are designed for worship, not for art studios. The layout does not have the open, flexible spaces that artists need, and renovations to adapt the space could be difficult. Limited natural light and ventilation will be an issue. You guys need bright, well-ventilated spaces for painting."

"I wish," muttered Dazzle to himself. He could imagine himself sitting near the door with some of the best light in the building, painting to his heart's delight. He looked around and could imagine the buzz of holidaymakers coming in and leaving with arms full of purchases. Then he came back down to earth and concentrated on proceedings.

Richard continued, "Chapels typically have large, open interiors that are costly to heat, especially in the colder months. Again, you guys working with paints, wood, or clay may struggle with temperature-sensitive materials. Coastal areas are humid, and chapels aren't always insulated for year-round use, potentially affecting the longevity of stored artworks and materials. I'm just laying out some issues you might like to consider that may not have crossed your minds."

An arm went up and Richard stopped.

"Please can you tell us what all this is going to cost us each week?" asked Daisy, a familiar attendee on the sea wall every Sunday, complete in her brightly coloured woven long coat and distinctive bobble hat.

"Sorry, but no. Until we have all the details of rent, power, water rates, council taxes and the like, our estimations could be wildly out. I do, however, promise that as soon as we do then we will share the figures with you," explained Richard.

Daisy thanked him.

"Now, where was I? Oh, yes, you will have to take the locals along with your ideas as some communities may feel protective of their chapel's historical or religious significance. They could resist certain activities, exhibitions, or events that they perceive as disruptive or disrespectful."

The audience nodded, which encouraged Richard to carry on.

"The chapel is not currently equipped with the plumbing or electrical capacity to support an artist collective. Studios often need sinks, reliable electricity, and workstations that can handle different types of equipment, but I have to say this chapel is in the most amazing location. With a frontage looking out to sea on a busy promenade, rain will be your friend and cold weather will be your ally to drive the customers in. I relish the thought of winning this on your behalf for a social enterprise."

Dazzle noticed his fellow artists glancing and nodding at each other, and a few of them whispered comments. It seemed they believed, for the first time, that the rain could be their friend and the cold weather, an ally.

"Now, about the collective," said Richard, commanding silence again. "The dynamics of people sharing space can be challenging and will require strong communication. Issues may arise over the allocation of zones, cleaning duties, and use of common areas. Artists may have different visions for the space, and conflicts could arise over its aesthetic direction, or the types of events held, requiring regular meetings and a clear structure for decision making. You all need to be aware of these points and be prepared to be flexible and tolerant from the start. However, despite all these challenges, with careful planning, community engagement, and creative problem solving, I honestly believe this group of artists could transform this hardly used chapel into a vibrant gallery hub offering valuable spaces for creative collaboration here on the south coast."

There was a round of applause, much to Richard's obvious amusement. Dazzle felt optimistic for the first time in a long time.

"From a personal point of view," Richard continued, after settling the group back down, "I believe you have the best location in which I have ever been involved. I believe the town council will applaud your initiative, and you will have the community behind you... as long as you serve very good coffee and piping hot teacakes with lashings of butter and strawberry jam at a fair price. Now, any questions?"

"What happens if I can't pay my share of the rent one month?" asked Penny, an oils artist who Dazzle recognised as another regular on the sea wall on Sundays in her duffle coat.

"It will probably happen to many of you if you have a bad month. However, when you have a good month, you can pay more into the funds to see you through the bad times. It's November, January and February I assume you're speaking about?"

"Yes," Penny replied. "It's a bad time for all of us."

There was a consensus of agreement from the group.

"What happens if one of us goes sick? Will all of our paintings be put out on to the street?" asked one of the few potters in the chapel.

"No, other ventures of this nature are managed by a small group of artists who make decisions on behalf of everyone. Here's an example where an artist was to be hospitalised for twelve weeks. Their space was rented out temporarily to another artist on the strict understanding that when the poorly artist was well enough to return, the temporary incumbent moved out immediately and the recovered artist moved back in. The whole group helped with both changes."

"What's in it for you?" shouted a suspicious voice from the back.

"Good question," said Richard. "I'm an artist myself, but I'm not good enough to compete with you guys. I have other skills like bid writing for grants and funding, which I'll bet diamonds is your worst nightmare."

"So, what's the next step?" Dazzle finally piped up.

"Well, we find out if the chapel is listed, if the council will support the venture, and who the movers and shakers in the ecclesiastical world are – only on one day a week, remember. Fortunately, I already know the decision makers in the local authority planning office. May I suggest you all go away and decide if you want to be part of this exciting new venture, and then we'll meet up next Sunday – same time, same place?

Nods and murmurs of approval were forthcoming, and an enthusiastic round of applause came spontaneously from the audience.

"Well, thank you for that," said Richard. "Unexpected applause always makes me look around to see if the real speaker has arrived."

Dazzle stood up, thanked Richard for his contribution, and waited for everyone's attention. He could hear Yorrie's warning ringing in his ears and said, "Just before we all go, I have a serious request. Please, please don't talk to anyone about our plans, for as soon as it becomes common knowledge that the chapel will be coming up for sale, everyone and their dog will want to convert it into another fast-food outlet, another rock shop, or knock it down for posh flats."

A mumbled agreement rippled through the audience.

As the meeting broke up, Dazzle was pleased to sense the positive vibes in the chatter as his fellow artists streamed out of the chapel.

Yorrie nudged him. "See, didn't I tell you, Daz? I knew they'd all be up for the idea. You've got a real tidy bunch of artists here."

17

Sitting on the platform waiting for the London train, Deborah stroked her Antler wheeled case then looked at Yorrie's duffle bag.

"Is that all you are taking?" she asked incredulously.

"It's all I've got," said Yorrie flatly. "Toothbrush and toothpaste, my AC/DC T-shirt, three socks that I rotate and a Fair Isle woolly my mam knitted, for if it gets cold."

"Pants?" Deborah queried.

"Wearing them, aren't I? Right way round today, back to front tomorrow, inside out right way round day three, and inside out and back to front day four."

Deborah's eyes went skyward.

The train pulled into the station, and they boarded. The train lurched into motion before they had found their seats. Rocking, they worked their way through the carriage.

When they reached their pre-booked seats and table, four men were already sitting there.

Deborah examined her tickets. Frowning, she said, "Excuse me, but I think you're sitting in two of our seats facing the engine."

"Find some other seats, darling," said one of the men without looking up.

"No," said Deborah flatly.

"There'll be loads of empty seats further along," he said, waving his hand absently towards the front of the carriage.

"No!" repeated Deborah firmly.

Yorrie started to move forward, but Deborah gave him an 'I'll deal with this' look, stopping him in his tracks.

She put her luggage down and reiterated, "You seem to be sitting in our pre-booked seats."

"Listen, darling–" started the first man again.

One of the other men looked up and immediately said, "Sorry for the mistake, Ma'am, we'll move right away."

Aghast, the first man said, "No we bloody well won't!"

He finally looked up and turned ashen. "I apologise for the misunderstanding Ma'am," he said, bundling all his papers together. He exited the seat and made his way down the carriage. The other three followed meekly.

Deborah, and a very impressed Yorrie, slid into their reserved seats.

"Just exactly how did you do that?" asked Yorrie. Her old nickname 'Fang' came to mind.

"I nicked two of them some years ago. I expect they are recently out on parole. The very last thing they need is an altercation on a train with me going on their record. Now let's enjoy the ride," replied Deborah nonchalantly, turning her head to look out of the window.

Yorrie shook his head in astonishment, having narrowly avoided a confrontation as his automatic solution. "Wow, I'm so proud to be with you," he said.

She turned back and smiled at him. "What a lovely thing to say, thank you," she replied, taking hold of his hand.

They began their journey from the southern coast of England up to London. At first, the view was filled with the open, salty blue of the sea with seagulls drifting lazily in the sky. Then, with the coast well behind them, the train ran through Hampshire's countryside, passing historic towns and villages rich with Georgian and Victorian architecture. It wove between forests and open fields. Trackside Buddleia, the butterfly bush, with its white or mauve flowers and bright red rosebay-willowherb, otherwise called fireweed or Ivan's chai, passed in a blur.

Further north, the train entered the Surrey Hills, an area of outstanding natural beauty. Yorrie pointed out dense woodlands, meadows, and picturesque small towns. The quieter, green landscapes soon made way for suburbs and commuter towns as they approached Greater London. The areas changed into a blend of residential homes, parks, and clusters of shops and businesses, giving a sense of the widespread commuter belt.

Deborah asked, "How did you travel from North Wales all the way down to the south coast?"

"Hitch-hiked, didn't I. However, if I recall correctly, there was way more hiking than hitching."

"How long did it take you?"

"About a week I think," said Yorrie.

"Have you travelled by train much?"

Yorrie nodded. "Yes, we went as a family on the North Wales rattler to Barmouth regularly."

Deborah smiled.

About thirty minutes from London, the scenery shifted noticeably to an urban landscape. Tracks multiplied, stations become more frequent, and the architecture began to reflect the city's spread with taller buildings, Victorian terraced houses, and industrial sites on both sides.

The train flew through iconic London boroughs, one after the other, each with their unique identity. The final stretch was defined by densely packed buildings, railway arches, and graffiti-covered walls; a sure sign they were nearing the city's heart.

Soon London began to reveal itself: modern apartment blocks, commercial headquarters, parks bordered by leafy trees, and a growing energy in the air. The city's square mile of skyline came into view, and they knew they were in the heart of the capital, where centuries old buildings mixed with modern skyscrapers.

Finally, they pulled into London Bridge station. As they rose from their seats, the four men from earlier stood back to allow them both to alight first.

One of them said, "Sorry for my mates earlier, Ma'am. Try as I might, I just can't educate pork."

Deborah smiled knowingly.

Yorrie's eyes were everywhere. The hotel was bigger than any building he had ever been in, and the room's view stretched across London. He was in awe of Deborah's generosity.

That evening, they went down to dinner but were stopped by the head waiter. He coughed then addressed Yorrie. "Excuse me, sir, but the restaurant is formal dress only tonight."

Deborah took the reins. "I'm sure while we are having a drink at the bar, a suitable jacket could be loaned on this occasion."

The waiter bowed his head. "Certainly, madam."

"I don't want a fuss; you go into the restaurant, and I'll get a bag of chips somewhere," said Yorrie.

"No, you are with me, and we shall dine together," replied Deborah.

The head waiter returned, interrupting their discussion. "Is this what you are looking for, madam?"

He held up a tartan jacket and Yorrie tried it on for size. It fitted perfectly.

"What do you think?" asked Yorrie, spinning around.

"I think the rest of the band will be coming later," she joked.

They both laughed and Yorrie thanked the head waiter, who left them to intercept other inappropriately dressed miscreants.

Yorrie turned to Deborah with a serious expression. He asked, "Can I keep it? I think I look pretty cool in it. What about you?"

"Thank you, no. Two things: it's not my size and I feel better in a dress and stole."

Yorrie smiled. "You do look amazing, you know, but what's with the stole indoors? My old dad used to say that a scarf was an item of clothing that a child has to wear when its mother gets cold."

Deborah raised her eyebrows. "Did your father really say all the things you say he said?"

"What, you doubt me?" retorted Yorrie, mock-astounded at the slight. "My dad said every word as surely as my name is Iorworth Llewellin ap Jenkins-Sandalwick-Crump... the second. Direct descendant of Owen Glyndwr, Prince of Wales, who had six sons and eight daughters. My mam says she's sure I'm related to the youngest son Gruffudd ap Owen Glyndwr, who was the runt of the litter."

The two howled with laughter as only lovers can and made their way to their table.

While Yorrie was examining the size of the wine glasses and excessive number of knives and forks, Deborah suggested that the next day could be spent in a mix of sightseeing and a short meeting with A. B. Chevron.

"I likes the idea of seeing some of the London sights, but there's no way must I have anything to do with meeting A. B. Chevron. Dazzle would never forgive me. Would you mind having the meeting without me?"

"No problem, but we ought to discuss what we need to get out of the meeting," said Deborah. "I believe we left it that they were going to find out who the two finders are, how they get the paintings to Susan, and what she does with them. If you remember, we gave them the P.O. box number."

"Yes – 20779715."

"Amazing memory, just amazing," commented Deborah, while pouring more red wine.

———

The next day, while Yorrie took himself for a wander around Chelsea, Deborah was knocking on the door of A. B. Chevron's offices.

The company receptionist introduced Deborah to Bernadette Westerman, the managing director, a smart business woman in a pinstriped suit. Coffee was offered and they sat in comfy chairs in the spacious board room. After the pleasantries, Bernadette started the meeting,

"Thank you for coming Miss Archer, it's always good to put a face to a telephone call. This case seems to have moved from one art dealer who isn't paying one painter into something much bigger. I had no idea it would grow like this." Bernadette took a swallow of coffee and continued, "I have put two more associates on your case. I'm afraid the final invoice will be bigger than we first discussed."

Deborah chose a biscuit and said, "Correct me if I am wrong but isn't there a European reward process set up for instances of this nature?"

"You are well informed, Miss Archer. There is, but it is notoriously difficult to access. However, we carefully document every move we make for the final report. Our policy is to share any reward with our clients on a fifty-fifty basis. Are you in agreement to proceed?"

"Certainly," confirmed Deborah, selecting another biscuit.

"Very well. We discussed the concept of 'finders' recently, and now we have some more info on how the scam works. The first finder is a retired man of very good reputation in the art world. He appears to find art for Susan Cartwright for pin money and the opportunity to travel around the UK, on expenses, doing what he loves. His name is Cedric Perkins. He's in his early sixties, unmarried, and was a painter of no mean stature in watercolour circles himself. The second finder is named Justin Caldwell. The Lothario of this case. A youngish man who seems to be very successful with women artists, who fall over themselves to supply paintings for him for no reward. Well, no *financial* reward. Some female artists are thought to have sent six paintings via Justin before realising it's a scam."

Deborah was on the edge of her seat. She was desperate to ask questions but decided not to interrupt Bernadette's flow.

"The two finders send the first paintings they have 'bought' to one P.O. box number. After either one or two paintings have been paid for in cash by the finders, the artists are then asked to send further paintings directly to another P.O. box number. There appears to be virtually no contact between Susan Cartwright and Cedric Caldwell or Susan Cartwright and Justin Perkins. I imagine that's to ensure there is no audit trail," Bernadette continued,

"So how does Susan Cartwright make any money?" asked Deborah, unable to help herself.

"That's the interesting part. Well, let's assume one of her finders pays cash for two paintings. For ease of the maths, let's say for £150 each. Outgoings £300. The unsuspecting, excited artist is then asked to send two more paintings but receives no recompense for those. Cartwright now has four paintings for £300, which works out at £75 each."

Deborah nodded.

"So, still seduced by the assurance that their first four paintings are on display in an upmarket gallery in London, the unsuspecting artist sends two more paintings without recompense before realising they have been duped. Cartwright now has six paintings for £300 – £50 each. Her partner, Hustletti, arranges for the paintings to be taken to a central place in London and sells them into the lucrative European market place for say £350 each. That works out at £2,100 total. A clear profit of £1,800 from each artist."

Deborah shook her head at the simplicity of the scheme. "Flattery and seduction are the only tools required to make an artist part with their work when struggling to make ends meet?"

"You're right. Obviously, there will be some expenses, and two finders will want a split, but if you scale up the operation for a couple of years then it becomes a very lucrative industry. The main benefit is that there is no connection between Cartwright or Hustletti and any of the artists. If questioned, Susan can honestly say that she does not know the artists, has never met any of them, and has never seen any of their paintings. Clever, eh?"

"Very," said Deborah, and sipped her coffee thoughtfully. Then she asked, "Have any of the artists ever attempted to go to the gallery or inform the police?"

Bernadette shook her head. "Our connections in the police do not believe anyone has tried to pursue the fraudsters. It takes money to undertake an investigation of this nature, and these artists are living from hand to mouth. They neither have the money or the time to chase their stolen paintings. Our associates have other thoughts too," continued Bernadette. "Initially, we assumed there were only two finders. But the number of paintings being delivered to the first P.O. box suggests there may be many more operating in the UK – further north, Scotland and the south east – and multiplying the output."

"And what about beyond the UK?" asked Deborah.

"Indeed. Our associates believe that this scam is about to be set up in Europe too. Where is Hustletti from? Italy. How long has he been out of prison? Three years. That's his link. By the way, Hustletti only communicates with the outside world via a small betting shop in Westminster called 'Honest John's'. The owner shared a cell with Hustlleti. Behind Honest John's is a substantial warehouse. It's there that the paintings are received, unwrapped, seen, repacked and couriered via container to various places in Europe, like Italy."

"Very interesting," murmured Deborah. "What do you advise we do next if we want to get the money back for a particular artist?"

Bernadette sighed. "Getting money back for a particular artist will be well-nigh impossible. The best will be to get their paintings back, but even the chance of that is very slim. I will need to consult with my associates. We don't want to scare Cartwright, Hustelleti or Honest John off. This afternoon we have a case review meeting here with a number of people involved in this case. We'll discuss it, then contact you tomorrow morning."

"Thank you, I look forward to your call."

———

In a café in Chelsea, Yorrie was talking to some hippie-style customers over a cup of coffee. He was explaining all about the adventures of being a cartographer in North Wales. They had never met a cartographer before. In fact, they had never met anyone from Wales before.

They were high, so they listened with that lovely, courteous, soporific look about them.

As Deborah arrived, Yorrie stood up and started to introduce her to his new friends.

"This is Deborah she's an ex-Chief–"

"Ex-friend if we miss the theatre tonight!" she quickly interjected. "And the price of tickets these days is extortionate!"

Yorrie picked up a collection of bags and the two of them left the café.

"I was just going to say–" he began.

"Well don't!" Deborah cut him off again. "Too many around here still bear a huge grudge against me for putting their relatives away for years. Remember the four men on the train? That situation was about three years ago, OK?"

"I was just excited to introduce you. Sorry," said Yorrie.

She threaded her arm into his, their spat over, and they began walking back to the hotel briskly.

Yorrie chatted about his morning, making her laugh at the things he had found remarkable. "I must show you what I brought for myself. London's an amazing place."

"I told you so," said Deborah, and smiled.

The next morning Deborah took the call from Bernadette, only to be told that her associates working on the case had underestimated the size of the outfit.

She told Deborah, "It appears that there are about six finders working in the UK. They were unable to give an exact figure for Europe. We need to obtain real evidence about the scam. On the advice of my associates, I have asked if it would be possible to insert a state-of-the-art tracker into the corner of the next painting that is due to be sent to the P.O. box number."

Deborah looked at Yorrie, who was also listening. He nodded.

"Yes, I suppose so," confirmed Deborah.

"Would you also be able to photograph the painting with the original artist's signature on it?"

Deborah looked at Yorrie, who nodded again. Deborah relayed this.

Bernadette continued, "As soon as you dispatch the painting, then please inform us and we'll look out for it. Once the painting arrives at the P.O. box it will be tracked. It will probably go on to Honest John's warehouse and then on to Italy, its final destination. We believe this evidence would be enough to go to the British police. Interpol could then coordinate the next step. One of our A. B. Chevron operatives will pop around to your hotel now with the tracker and explain how to use it."

After some more discussion about the minutia of the exercise, the call was ended.

"We're on then," said Deborah to Yorrie, clearly relishing the chase as she poured herself a coffee.

"Sounds like it," said Yorrie, pleased he was with her, and that they were one step closer to helping Dazzle.

18

The chapel was still warm from the Sunday evening service as the artists began to arrive for the second meeting to discuss Yorrie's idea of leasing the chapel when it was closed. At first, both Yorrie and Dazzle were nervous as the numbers were low – very low.

It was Richard Green who reminded them of who they were counting on. "Artists appear to have three speeds: dead slow, stop and 'Oh, sorry, I forgot.' They will come but most probably haven't owned a watch for years and those who do, won't have an hour hand on them. They will come, trust me, have faith."

There were about only eight artists sat down for a 7.30 p.m. start.

"I think they will come in dribs and drabs, as my old mam used to say," said Yorrie enthusiastically.

Just then, four more artists arrived, then two more, then seven came in ones and twos. Apologising for their tardiness, the additions to the group sat down nosily.

Richard Green asked, "Shall we make a start then?" He began reiterating the objective of the meeting just as another group of six jumbled through the door. There was a pause while they found seats, then the meeting continued.

It was after this that Dazzle nudged Yorrie and Deborah. When he had their attention, he asked, "Who are the two people in the second row?"

Yorrie and Deborah strained to see who Dazzle had pointed out.

"They're developers," said Deborah. "They work all along the south coast buying up old properties and turning them into posh flats. We need to get them out."

During a pause in the proceedings, Dazzle whispered in Richard's ear, relaying the information.

"Leave it to me," Richard said quietly.

Returning to face the audience he began, "Right, now, I would like you all to decide if you are a disciple of the plan. If you are, move over to sit here, please." He pointed to the left-hand side of the chapel. "If you are an agnostic and want some more time and information to make up your mind, please sit in the middle of the chapel. And if you are an atheist and really unsure of the plan, please sit on the right-hand side of the chapel."

A lot of noise preceded the movement. He then said very loudly, "And the fourth group of non-artists and developers are asked to leave this private meeting and make a group of their own outside."

All the artists stopped and looked around to see who had not moved. Slowly but surely, the two embarrassed developers made their way to the back of the chapel accompanied by catcalls, boos, whistles and cries of shame.

Once the developers had gone, Richard counted up the groups.

"There appear to be five atheists, ten agnostics and twelve disciples. In front of you are some flip charts. Please split into groups of five or four and discuss your dreams and your fears for the gallery. Please don't hold back. If we know your dreams, we can direct our energy to achieving them. If we know your fears, we can work towards allaying them, or you may well have spotted something we have missed."

Dazzle, Yorrie, Deborah and Richard moved amongst the groups encouraging openness and frankness. Lots of laughter filled the normally quiet chapel. After thirty minutes of noise and conversation, the pages from the flip charts were brought to the front, pinned up and discussed openly. Some artists suggested the discussions had helped them move their thinking from atheists to agnostics. Some agnostics agreed and had moved to disciples following the discussions.

The exercise had achieved its objective of getting everyone talking, everyone knowing each other, and raising the level of enthusiasm for the gallery. Richard collected the flip charts and said he would bring them back next time.

He concluded by imparting the information he had been tasked to find out at the last meeting. "I have found out that the chapel is not listed, thank goodness. Very informally, I have found out the town council would be in favour of such a plan. I could find no movers and shakers in the ecclesiastical world who would help us. Sorry, I failed there. But I did informally discuss your proposal with the decision makers in the local authority planning office, one of whom is studying for her degree in mixed media art. I think we should invite her to our next meeting. And on that note, would you like to meet up again next week?"

There was a resounding 'yes' from the audience.

"I suggest we have one person for all the communications to go through. May I propose it is Dazzle?" asked Brian dreadlocks in his blue, faded fisherman's top.

It was a unanimous vote.

When the chapel was empty, Dazzle, Yorrie, Deborah and Richard sat down to discuss the evening and the way forward.

"They are really excited!" exclaimed Yorrie. "If we don't pull this off, we'll all have to move, or risk being tarred and feathered."

"Yes, the developers being here was a real wake up call to the artists and to us. They will be moving quicker than we can, if we're not careful," Yorrie suggested.

Richard suggested he and Dazzle should go to the church commissioner's office the following week to try to get in first. They all agreed.

Deborah said that she would talk to 'some people' too. Nobody asked who specifically, for they all knew she was well connected.

"By the end of the meeting, I believe there were three atheists, five agnostics and up to nineteen disciples. Another meeting like tonight and the numbers will be even greater!" said an animated Dazzle. "Perhaps we could convert them all," he said excitedly.

19

"Not on your life am I sending any more paintings to Susan," said Dazzle on Monday following the meeting. "She didn't even have the courtesy to say she wasn't coming last weekend, neither did she thank me for the last painting," grumbled Dazzle. "And as for payments, I might as well be whistling in the wind. Have you any idea what she owes me? I'm such a fool. I should have stopped sending them when she didn't pay me the first time, but I was worried I'd upset her. Well, she can get stuffed as far as I'm concerned."

"As my old dad used to say, 'Don't torch the ship you're hoping to sail on,'" said Yorrie.

"What's that supposed to mean?" snapped Dazzle.

"It means, from one point of view, you were, and still are, hoping to enjoy a long-term relationship with Susan. From another point of view, she has offered to sell your paintings at twice the price you are currently getting for them. And from a third point of view, if she walked through that door right now, you would be all over her like a rash, isn't it?" he suggested.

"Well, I would have some months ago, but now I'm not so sure," he replied. Then, after thinking about it for a moment, admitted, "Well, yes, I suppose I would even now, you're right."

"And going back to the second point of view, I can't remember you mentioning a queue of folk offering to sell your paintings for you. In fact, I can't remember anyone, offering anything... ever."

Dazzle grunted in agreement.

"Well, for what it's worth," said Yorrie, "I think you should send one more painting to Susan with a note saying you are looking forward to seeing her soon." He began collecting the dirty cups in the room. "But I'm Welsh, what do I know?"

With that, he stomped off into the kitchen to wash up.

A full ten minutes went by before Yorrie came back into the lounge. Time that Dazzle had clearly spent thinking.

"Do you really believe I should send one more?" he asked hesitantly.

"Yep. To know for certain, as the song goes, so just follow your heart not your wallet."

"OK, but this is the very last one, for definite."

"There you go again!" exploded an exasperated Yorrie. "Being mega negative, surrounding your paintings with black thoughts. Susan will reflect back to you exactly your level of expectancy. You expect Susan to dismiss your note, you expect her to decline your request to see her, you're cross with her. Sending anger and irritation will be returned by her in spades. You mark my word, boyo."

Dazzle seemed too taken aback by Yorrie's passion to interrupt.

"But on the other hand, sending her love and your genuine feelings for her will be returned in equal measure, isn't it? At this moment, all the vibes that travel with your paintings are angry vibes." Yorrie contorted his mouth into a snarl to emphasise the thought.

"Mega grumpy vibes. Stop! Change your mind set, Daz. Get as far away from your seething temper as you can. I had a mate back home who could walk into a room where things were simmering and turn it to boiling in a minute just by his vibes, just like you. You're transparent, Daz, that's what you are." Yorrie nodded to himself at the memory of his mate.

"What about the good times you and Susan had? Think about the laughter and the dinners you enjoyed together, drinking and the like. Think about waking up and cwtshing her in the mornings. A great feeling, I'll be bound." Yorrie was in top gear, conscious he needed Dazzle to send one more painting to the scammers. "So, construct a note to go with the painting, something warm and genuine. Definitely not slushy. Dab in and write something honest, frank and sincere while I wrap up the painting ready to send."

Yorrie could tell Dazzle still wasn't sure, but he agreed to go with the positivity suggestion. He went up to his room to write the note. As soon as he was out of sight, Yorrie brought out Deborah's camera and took several photos of Dazzle's signature in the bottom right-hand corner of the painting. He then secretly inserted the tracker in the wooden frame of the canvas as he had been shown by the A. B. Chevron employee. Next, he wrapped it up in exactly the same way he had seen Dazzle wrap his paintings previously.

A short while later, Dazzle came downstairs and passed Yorrie his note.

"Cracking, Daz, I can feel the warmth from here," encouraged Yorrie. It was the last thing to be included, and the package was finally sealed.

"I just hope you're right," said Dazzle.

"'Course I'm right. Positivity, that's what you need, and buckets full of it I've got. I've a good feeling about this painting," said Yorrie, stroking it after putting on his familiar denim jacket. "I'll take the package to the post office on my way to Deborah's."

———

"The painting has gone and here's your camera," said Yorrie when he was settled in Deborah's lounge. "Several snaps I took to make sure we had a really good, focussed one. I hope that was all right?"

"Of course, and the tracker?" asked Deborah.

"Safely tucked inside the frame, and before you ask, yes, I switched it on. Will you let A. B. Chevron know it's safely on its way?"

"Of course," she said again, leaning across to give him a peck on the cheek. "He is lucky to have a friend like you."

"Let's hope he feels the same way when all this hits the fan."

———

That night, the painting, complete with the electronic tracker, began its short journey to London by train.

Two days later it was transported, in a Royal Mail van, to P.O. box 20779715 to await collection in Chelsea.

Outside the Chelsea post office, a non-descript builder's van was parked. It housed one of A. B. Chevron's people whose listening equipment was scanning for the reassuring electronic tracker. Once picked up, a phone call was made to Bernadette Westerman.

"Wait and see who collects the painting and follow it to its destination," was the instruction.

Two hours later, a black estate car parked opposite the post office. Its driver loaded the painting into the back along with six more packages of varying sizes.

The A. B. Chevron driver, at a safe distance behind, followed the black estate car and parked forty yards down the road, on the opposite side to Honest John's betting shop. He watched as six paintings being unloaded and taken inside.

He was just about to drive off when the tracker indicated it was on the move again. The driver could only assume Dazzle's painting was still inside the estate car and being driven east.

Eventually, the black estate car stopped, the painting was removed and taken to a three-story townhouse on Horseferry Street. After a brief exchange with the estate car's driver, a blond woman in her mid-forties took the wrapped parcel inside the house.

The A. B. Chevron driver returned to Honest John's and took some photos of the container in the yard through the fence. Fortunately, it was facing the correct way, and all the signage was clear.

Susan Cartwright carefully unwrapped the painting and put the note from Dazzle into her pocket to read later.

She surveyed the painting under various lights in the high-ceilinged drawing room and said to Giacomo, "This is probably his best work yet. I'm amazed he still keeps sending them to me. I feel really bad; he was such a nice guy. How I hate what we do sometimes."

Giacomo threw her a glance. "Don't you start going soft on me now. I told and told you not to go and see him last time, but you would have it your way. Don't forget you had a crap journey there and he was as pissed as a rat when you arrived. Now you feel bad because you're cheating him out of just a few grand. That doesn't make any sense," he ranted. "None of the other artists mean anything to you but you've bled them all dry. You couldn't leave him alone. You wouldn't listen to me, would you? You had to go and fall for this guy. Send him a note that says it's all over and you're now happily married with six kids and another on the way. That should cool him off a bit."

Giacomo sat down heavily into one of the high-backed wing chairs, shaking his head. "Why am I getting nervous about you and this guy Drizzle or whatever his name is?"

"Shut up, Giacomo, and look at his painting. We really are selling his work too cheaply. I think we should raise the price to over a £1,000 when we sell it on or keep one or two like this back till the market is crying out for his work. People will pay double."

"No, definitely not. Our business model is very successful and based on simple turnover, not individual paintings," said Giacomo. He stood up and went over to the sideboard to fill his crystal whisky glass with single malt.

He continued, "As soon as we veer away from our model, we become vulnerable. Just let the painting go with the rest and stay on track. And before you ask, no you can't keep it. Why, do I say you can't keep it? Because every time you look at it, you'll consider getting back in touch with him and that's a slippery slope. You'll establish an audit trail as wide as a motorway back to us. No, definitely not, you can't keep it. Tomorrow, I'll take it to John's for distribution with all the rest. We have a container nearly full, and it will be on the move to Italy in a couple of weeks."

"Look, Giacomo, I would buy that painting if I saw it on a sea wall in the south of England. I would buy it without hesitation. He's good, bloody good. Out of the hundreds of paintings we move I want one. This one."

Giacomo took a big drink of the neat spirit. It burned the back of his throat, and he coughed. "No, definitely not. Every artist in history had to be dead long before they were recognised, right? Well, in view of the fact that you taught him in short pants in the sixth form, that makes him much younger than you. So, you will be long gone before he becomes famous. Straight forward arithmetic. The painting goes tomorrow." He dismissed the idea with a wave.

Sulking, Susan continued to move the painting around the poorly lit room to get the best of what little light there was, trying to ignore what Giacomo had said. Eventually, he said good night to her. She told him she wanted another drink to help her sleep but the real reason was to stay downstairs, close to Dazzle. She wanted time to think. She kept questioning herself. If he wasn't a really good artist, would she have any feelings for him, say if he was a banker? She thought not, but he was a first-class painter in a world that she knew well, on top of which she *did* have feelings for him, more than she cared to admit.

Susan poured herself a large gin and tonic, adding two massive ice cubes and a sliver of lemon. She retrieved Dazzle's note and, after plumping up some scatter cushions, settled down in her favourite chair. The note read:

My dear Susan,
As I write this, I find myself thinking about you and how much I've missed you. The days without you feel longer, lonelier, and very quiet. It's no wonder for all I have to fill my days are Yorrie and his dad's bloody sayings.
Lately, though, I find myself caught in moments of uncertainty, questioning whether the distance between us is simply physical or if something else is pulling us apart. It's a thought I wrestle with. How about you?
I love the time, the laughter and the dreams we've shared. They are a continual reminder of why I hold you so dear, even when uncertainty colours my thinking.
Please help me understand how you feel. If my worries are unfounded, I'd love to know, and if they aren't unfounded, I believe we owe it to each other to speak honestly. I cherish what we've had and would hate for it to drift into a silence of misunderstanding.
No matter where we stand, please know you've been a huge influence in my life – at school and recently. I'm grateful for every moment we've had. I hope we can find a way to bridge this distance – whatever form it takes – and rediscover the closeness that has always meant so much to me.
With love,
Dazzle
Xxx

Susan put the letter down, took a big drink, and looked at the painting again with wet eyes. How could she get herself out of the situation with Giacomo much earlier than planned and connect again with Dazzle, she wondered? Her relationship with Giacomo was purely work and she mused that she should have left the scam long ago and settled down with Dazzle. In fact, as soon as she met Dazzle again.

However, Giacomo had all the connections in London and Italy, and she had the money to fund the scam. Now she had too much time and money invested to pull out. If she did, her house and gallery would both become vulnerable as they were heavily linked to the scam.

She didn't trust Giacomo to keep quiet about the part she played if he was caught, and Honest John also knew all about her. There was no way she could extricate herself without leaving a trail that even a blind man could follow.

She thought for a while, not looking at anything in particular, and took another swallow of the powerful gin. What if she wrapped another painting up to give to Giacomo in the morning and kept Dazzle's in her room? That would make her feel closer to him.

She and Giacomo had decided that when this container of paintings had been dispatched, they would work on the final container and then split all the income. Honest John would take over the business. She would sell her house in Westminster and the Chelsea gallery and move Antigua. Giacomo would move to Italy.

There would be no contact between the three of them ever again. That was the plan.

The gin wasn't helping; it was making her thinking fuzzy. The time frame for the termination of the business was three months. Could she wait that long? More importantly, would Dazzle wait for another three months? If the roles were reversed, would she have even waited till now? Absolutely not!

Finishing her drink, she knew it was unwise to make any decisions tonight, for gin made her brave. Brave enough to write to him?

She collected a pen and pondered over a blank sheet of paper.

How on earth should she start?

> Dear Dazzle,
> Sorry, but I never had any intentions of paying you. We had a lot of fun. I know I haven't seen you for two months, but now things are going pear shaped around me here, I think I like you enough to try again.
> Lots of love,
> Susan
> xx

Or:

> My Dear Dazzle,
> I miss sleepy sex with you.
> Susan
> x

Four times she wrote a note and four times she tore it up in temper. Eventually she went off to bed.

Outside the house in Horseferry Street, the builders van had been replaced by a more sophisticated police surveillance vehicle parading as a motorway maintenance vehicle.

And all the time, the sinister signal from Dazzle's painting continued.

Susan rose early the next morning and confirmed her deliberations. She had decided to exchange Dazzle's painting for another less valuable painting of the same size. After breakfast, she handed over the swapped, repackaged painting to Giacomo.

As he went out to the black estate car, he turned back and said, "Thank you. It is in all our interests to keep to the plan on the side of turnover, and I am pleased you have come to your senses."

However, minutes later, a fuming Giacomo stormed back into the house holding the unwrapped painting. He demanded an explanation, stating she had broken his trust.

"We should stop now!" shouted Susan. "While we are ahead. Let's forget the last container. The jails are full of people who planned to commit 'just one more' crime, or rob 'just one more' bank, or set up 'just one more' fraud, vowing to retire afterwards. They all regret it now!"

"The jails are also full of stupid people who don't follow plans! We must stick to ours for another three months," Giacomo shouted. He picked up Dazzle's painting and stormed out to the estate car, which was driven off quickly.

———

Leaving a respectable distance between them, the police surveillance vehicle followed the black estate car down the road and out of sight.

———

The argument had convinced Susan that she should leave the scam sooner rather than later, whatever the cost financially. No doubt the argument had convinced Giacomo that Susan had become a liability too. She had to consider her next move carefully.

Stomping around, she swore and talked to herself.

Two coffees later, she had calmed down and her thinking was clearer. Her first call was to the estate agent handling the sale of her gallery. She gave him both barrels for his lack of progress. Susan blasted that if there was no action by the end of the week then she would change agents.

The next three calls were to residential estate agents. She asked each one to visit her home and give her a valuation. She arranged these for when Giacomo was out.

20

Dazzle and Richard sat silently listening to an ancient grandfather clock ticking noisily in the chapel's entrance. It sounded irritated by the unwelcome strangers and its tick-tock was getting perceptibly louder the longer they waited. Neither had noticed it previously during the two evening meetings with the artists.

Dazzle surveyed the surroundings of the chapel in the daylight. The carpet runner down the centre had threadbare patches at the main entrance and next to each row of pews. The shelves behind each pew had a thick layer of dust along their full length.

"Signs of the times," he said to Richard as he pointed at the carpet.

In its day, the chapel would have had an army of proud members who believed it was their duty to clean and polish every piece of wood and shine every piece of brass. In its heyday, he imagined the chapel would have been busy with toddler groups, Sunday school, and choir meetings, as well as the services.

Richard nodded knowingly. "It's my biggest concern."

Dazzle frowned. "I don't understand," he said.

Richard explained, "The chapel may have stacked up a load of debts in its dying years and the only way out now is a quick sale to the highest bidder."

Dazzle nodded; he knew they couldn't compete.

Expecting a dusty, white-haired, jumbling elder to meet them, they were surprised when a young man suddenly appeared. He shook their hands vigorously as if he was genuinely pleased to meet them.

"Hello, I'm Dave Thompson, one of the elders of the chapel." He ushered them into what he referred to as his 'office', which consisted of the front pew, and asked how he could help them.

Richard outlined their proposal of leasing the chapel and turning it into an art gallery, to support local artists. He explained that they did not know to whom they should make their proposal and asked where the central headquarters was based.

Dave listened intently. "Perhaps you are unfamiliar with how a Baptist chapel is governed?" he asked.

The two admitted they were.

"First, each place of Baptist worship is self-governed, in a bottom-up approach to decisions. Every member of the chapel has an equal say whether you are a minister, deacon, diakonissa, elder, or someone who takes on a leadership role like running the Sunday school or the choir. This applies to matters of finance too. In the case of this chapel, it has been decided by the members that we must not go into debt, however, currently, we are bouncing along close to the breakeven line. We are currently in a very precarious position. Are you following me?"

Dazzle and Richard both nodded.

Dave continued, "Well, only the other night, it was decided by the members that we must close the chapel as a place of worship for the number of members has dropped to our lowest level in the chapel's history. It will indeed be an unhappy day when we close our doors to worship. Sadly, we are not the only church or chapel facing such a dilemma in these times."

"When do you think that will happen?" queried Dazzle.

"Next month," confirmed Dave.

"Wow, as soon as that?" Dazzle was shocked.

"Yes. Remember, the decision was not to go into debt, but we are now nosediving towards debt. I must tell you that you are not the only group who have their eyes on the chapel. Two developers were here yesterday having a look around and asking questions. I understand even you had some interlopers in your meeting?"

Richard nodded again. Dazzle thought he looked pensive. A nervousness about competition for the chapel had settled on them both.

They discussed a possible lease, terms and conditions, as well as what would be included and what would not. Dazzle was so glad Richard was with him for he would have drowned at the pace of the conversation on his own. Eventually, a three-year lease was suggested by both sides and the principles would be put to the chapel members the following week.

Dazzle and Richard agreed they would get a decision from the artists as soon as possible. If all parties said yes, the legal paperwork would be drawn up for the chapel. They could be in within a month if all went well. The speed made them nervous.

Following the meeting in the chapel, Dazzle and Richard headed for a coffee shop to plan their next steps. Deep in conversation, they were surprised to look up and find two middle-aged, smartly dressed men standing behind them, a little too close for comfort.

The men asked if they could join them.

"Why?" asked Richard looking about at all the other empty tables.

The more senior of the two men started the conversation. "We noticed you coming out of the chapel and assumed you were making overtures to the elders about its future. We also have an interest in the chapel and wondered how serious you were in obtaining a lease or purchasing the chapel from its members."

Richard spoke, "I'm not sure our plans are any of your business. We're not going to talk to you or anybody else about them."

"Just having a chat, nothing sinister," said the man. Uninvited, he and his colleague both pulled out chairs and sat down. "You see, we would like to buy the chapel and develop it as a haven of upmarket flats for the holiday market."

Dazzle and Richard exchanged glances. Dazzle knew Richard was thinking the same thing: this was the competition against whom they could not compete.

The more senior man continued, "If there were no other bidders in the race it would save us some money, which we would be willing to share with you, if you know what I mean?"

"No, we don't know what you mean," said Richard, and took a drink of his coffee.

Dazzle was about to speak when Richard put his hand on his arm and asked, "Just exactly how much might it save you?"

The man replied, "It will save us about £2,000. That would be £1,000 each for you."

Dazzle shook his head. "I'm not listening to this. It sounds deceitful, unlawful and underhand. I'm off."

"Now don't be hasty," said the quieter of the two men. "How about we call it £2,000 each then?"

Richard stood up. "I'm off too," he said.

"OK, maybe I went in a little too low. How about £3,000 each?"

"See you around." Dazzle noisily pushed his chair out and stood next to Richard.

"Well, what would you want to pull out?" asked the exasperated quieter man.

"£5,000 each," said Richard.

"For me, you can shove your offer," snapped Dazzle, and started to walk away.

"Just sit down for a minute, Dazzle," said Richard.

Reluctantly, he did as he was told.

"How's this going to work then?" snapped Richard.

The quieter man said, "You pull out of the lease deal now by saying you've changed your mind, and we go ahead with our offer on the chapel. As soon as we have exchanged on the purchase, we put £5,000 in each of your bank accounts. The easiest money you will ever make."

Dazzle looked at Richard. Richard then said to the two men, "Thank you for your generous offer, gentlemen, but on reflection, you can shove your £10,000 where the sun doesn't shine. Good day."

They pushed back their chairs back again and walked out of the coffee shop. They hadn't gone ten yards down the street when the quieter man caught up with them. He held his palms up, asking them to stop.

"I'm afraid we haven't been entirely honest with you. May I introduce Gareth, a deacon of the chapel." He gestured to the senior man. "My name is Donald and I'm an elder of the chapel."

"Well, its's nice to meet you, but you can both f*** off with your deception," snapped Richard.

"I agree," said Dazzle.

The two of them kept walking.

"We understand how you feel, and we apologise to you both," called Donald.

Dazzle glanced at Richard. He sensed a complete change in the man's tone. They turned around.

"Please just listen?" asked Gareth.

"Go ahead," said Richard.

"When Dave Thompson said he was meeting with the two of you, we decided it was important to see if you were honourable people to pass on our beloved chapel to. There are members of our congregation who have had a lifelong association with the chapel. They were baptised there; they were married there, they ran the Sunday school there, and they are hoping to have their funeral services there. It has been central to their families for decades. We need to be able to assure them it will be in good hands, even in the short term. We hope you understand our concern."

"And?" queried a now calmer Richard.

"We will be confirming to the members of the chapel that you are both honourable people and recommending that they allow you and your artists to lease the chapel for three years."

"Well, thank you," said Dazzle. "We, for our part will set up another meeting with the artists and let you know if they wish to pursue the project. The majority were positive at the last meeting, depending on the costs."

"If it helps to persuade them, we would be prepared to let you have the chapel rent free for the first two months, to help you get off the ground. I'm sure we can persuade our members to make that allowance."

The four shook hands and agreed to get back together in one week's time.

———

That Sunday night in the chapel, Richard was able to assure Dave Thompson that nineteen of the artists had agreed to form an artist's consortium, which would be managed by

Dazzle and two of the other artists. They would sign the lease on behalf of the consortium. Another five had agreed to support the venture but couldn't commit to a regular lease payment. Three other atheist artists had wished the rest of them well, but unfortunately, for different personal reasons, they wouldn't be participating.

Following Richard's update, Dave Thompson addressed the silent audience of artists. He explained that there had been a meeting during the week and all the chapel members had voted to set up a lease with the artists. He outlined the costs. There was a round of applause and smiles.

The artists split up and discussed how to use the space most profitably. A smaller group discussed how a small café could be shoe-horned into the chapel without taking up too much valuable space. Deborah and Yorrie moved between the groups adding ideas. Richard suggested that a launch date was essential, otherwise talking would eat away at the two rent free months.

Dazzle, Richard and the group of artists all agreed to an impossibly tight deadline. One month after the lease was signed, they would have an opening for the chapel community followed the next day by a grand opening. Dazzle could sense the energy and enthusiasm in the chapel. He and his fellow struggling artists were feeling a passion they had not experienced for a while.

Towards the end of the meeting, it was time for Deborah to introduce her four visitors. Her first visitor was a solicitor who offered to oversee the legal aspects – insurances and art copyrights etc. – for no fee. The second visitor was a builder who offered to help advise and reorganise the interior – for no labour fees. Visitor number three was an accountant who offered to help set up a business plan, and the financial and operating systems – for no fee. And the fourth visitor was the managing director of a security company, who offered to help keep the place secure – for no labour fees.

After engaging in trivial discussions about the price to be charged for coffee, whether or not to sell biscuits, the colour scheme of the walls, the hours the gallery would be open, and who should do the cleaning, the group of artists listened carefully to the visitors, their embarrassment reddening their faces. Dazzle was thankful for Deborah and her connections. These four massively important tasks had clearly not even been considered by the audience, and to have them taken care of for no extra cost was amazing. The group stood up and applauded.

———

The next few weeks flew by for Dazzle. He was so inundated with questions and decision making on behalf of the artists' consortium and the chapel that he didn't even think about Susan.

"Can I start bringing my painting things, like my easel and frames for display this week?" asked Penny.

"No. There are two more Sunday services before we get the keys," replied Dazzle.

"Can I bring my dog?" Queried Brian dreadlocks.

"No. There are no animals allowed in the chapel according to the lease," stated Dazzle.

"Does the chapel have an urn for tea?" Asked someone from the café group.

"No idea." Dazzle shrugged.

And on and on came the questions.

Soon, it was time to consider the' legals': the lease from the solicitor, the maintenance contracts, operating instructions for the boiler, and agreements for the elders to have access to the chapel once it was operational. The responsibilities were piling up on him, but Dazzle loved it all. It was so exciting.

———

Four weeks later, on June 20th, the chapel was ready to open as promised. Deborah's professional connections had all done their bit and apart from a few of the artists, who took a more cavalier approach to deadlines in life, the gallery was ready. The chapel community were all invited to a pre-opening day which made them feel very special.

On the appointed day the mayor formally opened the gallery, and the café ran out of coffee and currant buns in the first hour, a measure of the need for a hub of this nature on the sea front. Dazzle was interviewed countless times by the local press. Garlands decorated the sea front, balloons waved at the visitors, and 150 holiday makers viewed the work of the local artists in the first morning.

Dazzle, Yorrie, Deborah, Richard and most of the artists had a party after the launch and toasted Dazzle's initiative. He was now recognised in the town as Mr. Dazzle, Gallery Manager.

21

"What's the problem today then, why so miserable?" asked Yorrie as he stirred that night's casserole.

Dazzle sighed heavily as he began to lay the tiny kitchen table. "Oh, same old niggle that I'm being tricked, deceived or misled by Susan. Am I that naive? Am I so gullible? I'm really not sure of anything now. I know I'm not seventeen anymore with a crush on my teacher. I'm nearly forty years old, for God's sake, and I've been around the block a few times. There's a difference in our ages but that disappeared on the first night, and the difference between our painting abilities has narrowed over time – Susan said so herself. She couldn't have faked all our time together, could she?"

Yorrie kept stirring the casserole, frequently tasting and adding tiny amounts of seasoning, letting Dazzle talk.

"Why do you keep adding just one grain of salt at a time?" asked a very irritable Dazzle as he placed the cruet and water glasses on the tabletop.

"'Cos my old mam used to say, 'You can always add, but you

can't take away.' She also said, 'It's such an insult to the chef when folk put salt and pepper on their food before tasting.'"

"Yeah, yeah, yeah. I know you mean me."

"If the cap–"

Without letting him finish Dazzle, returned to his earlier topic – Susan. "Do you think I'm being stupid? I haven't heard a word from her and that's despite the letter you made me write. What a waste of time that was. I've a jolly good mind to jump on a train, go to her art gallery, and have it out with her once and for all!"

Alarm bells started ringing in Yorrie's head. The last thing he, Deborah, A. B. Chevron or the police needed right now was for Dazzle to rock up in London asking questions and demanding to have his paintings back as well as the money he was owed.

Yorrie needed to play for enough time to allow the tracked painting to get to Italy

"Pass the dishes and I'll serve," he said.

When they had both sat down, Yorrie looked across at his forlorn landlord. "Now Daz, you can mope about because you think you've been dumped by Susan, or you can smile inwardly because you had the most amazing time with her that nobody can ever take away from you. What's it going to be eh?"

Between mouthfuls of casserole, dumplings and jacket potatoes, Dazzle chided, "You've changed your tune. Only last week you were all for me sending one more painting. 'Send her warm words, genuine and sincere' you said, and now you're saying I've been dumped." Dazzle poured water for both of them.

166

"It's neither," replied Yorrie calmly. "I don't know if you have been dumped or not, but I do know you could not have been more patient about the situation. If you haven't been dumped and Susan eventually offers a perfectly plausible explanation, then thank the Lord you didn't burn your ships."

Yorrie continued. "What I'm trying to gets across to you is that you're not looking forward at all. You're turning your back on tomorrow and all the amazing things that are in front of you. You appear to be trying to live in yesterday again and again and again. Susan may not be part of tomorrow because of the way she has treated you recently, so you must look forward to the future on your own. Your life may feel empty because you can't have her, but right now, you don't have her anyway, do you? Or you can be full of the love you shared even during the serious times and move on, wiser for the experience, isn't it?"

Yorrie could tell that Dazzle was listening carefully to every word. Surely, he knew it all made sense. He didn't have Susan right now so why was he expecting her to breeze back into his life? She wasn't coming back. Yorrie, for his part, was trying to let him down gently from what he already knew was happening with A. B. Chevron.

"So, it's either be miserable as sin every day, which rubs off on all those around you like me, Deborah, and all your customers," said Yorrie. "Or grasp the challenges of tomorrow, like the gallery and the twenty plus artists who are hanging on to your coattails and relying on you to drive it to astounding success. You have a fantastic future in front of you in the town as Mr. Dazzle, Gallery Manager."

With that, Yorrie poured their water away, retrieved two beers from under the sink, thought about it for a nanosecond, then retrieved two more. He opened two, poured them carefully into the glasses and came back to the table. There he chinked glasses with his landlord and said, "Here's to tomorrow, boyo."

22

The phone rang in Deborah's lounge. It was Bernadette from A. B. Chevron, calling with an update.

"Please thank your colleague for inserting the tracker in your local artist's painting. I can confirm that it arrived safely at the Chelsea P.O. box number. There the signal was picked up by one of our people and followed to Honest John's betting shop in London where a number of paintings were unloaded. Only one painting continued its journey to an address in Horseferry Street in London – the one with the tracker in it. The painting was handed over by the driver to a middle-aged blond woman who took it inside. At this point we informed the police who took over the surveillance task. The police reported that early the next morning the tracked painting was moved to Honest John's shop, where it was unloaded. The police checked the container sailing booking, which was for two weeks ahead. They assumed the container was waiting for more paintings."

"What happens next?" asked Deborah, knowing this new information meant they were beginning to home in on the scammers.

"The UK police have contacted their counterparts in Europe who will take over tracking the paintings to Italy. When enough evidence has been collected, they will pounce."

"What will you do in the meantime?"

"We have to be careful that we are not seen to be interfering in the police activities," said Bernadette. "However, they are really short of staff, so I think they will secretly be glad of any help they can get."

"What help do you suggest?" asked Deborah.

"I think we should go after the two finders – Cedric and Justin – next. If we could persuade them to let us have the names of some of the artists who have been scammed, even if it's just one or two, we could pass that info over to the UK police. At this moment in time, apart from your artist friend, we don't have any victims of the crime. We have about three weeks before the Italian police pounce."

"How about if my colleague and I take on one of the finders and A. B. Chevron takes on the other?"

Bernadette thought about this suggestion for a moment before she replied, which Deborah liked. "We do not work with any other organisations officially so the answer is no, thank you, but if you were to undertake some research into one of the finders, we could take over from there."

"We'll take on Cedric Perkins and keep you informed of what we find out," suggested Deborah.

"Please be careful, and no heavy-handed methods," pleaded Bernadette.

"Of course not," said Deborah, who had no intention of deploying unlawful methods.

"Then it's agreed."

Deborah put the phone down and immediately rang her old friend Bobby Sandwich of the Metropolitan Police stolen art recovery team.

"Good morning, Ma'am. How can I help you?" replied Bobby, recognising her voice immediately.

I wondered if you could do me a favour whilst you are having your coffee break–"

"I wish," he interrupted.

Deborah smiled wryly, remembering all too well how busy things used to be. "I wondered if you had come across a scam involving a guy called Giacomo Hustletti or a woman named Susan Cartwright?"

"Not heard of Susan Cartwright, Ma'am," Bobby answered straightaway, "but I wondered when Giacomo Hustletti would crawl out of the woodwork again. I nicked him way back. So, what's he been up to then? Could it be something to do with naive young artists being duped by the offer of their paintings hanging in a posey Chelsea gallery that my team have just got involved in?"

"I think so. He appears to be running the show this time rather than being the fall guy, which is what landed him in the nick last time," said Deborah. "What about Cedric Perkins? Apparently, he used to be an awesome watercolour artist himself back in the days but now goes about 'finding' gullible young artists for Giacomo," she explained.

Bobby thought for a few moments then expanded on Cedric, "Right, Perkins is about sixty and was a seasoned art connoisseur whose demeanour exuded a mix of charm and an air of quiet manipulation. Formerly an esteemed art judge with decades of experience critiquing and curating exhibitions. In his younger days, he was known for his sharp eye and eloquent art commentary. However, in the twilight of his career he now paints a murkier picture. Please excuse the pun."

"Go on," said Deborah.

"As I understand it, Ma'am, many years ago, he had an altercation at a judging event where copious levels of alcohol had been consumed. He retired from judging immediately. He now operates under the guise of 'a patron of emerging talent'. He persuades young, hungry artists, desperate for exposure, to send their work to a gallery in London, promising the allure of prestige and networking opportunities. The arrangement is steeped in imbalance as he never actually pays for their art. Instead, he relies on the artists' naivety and eagerness for recognition. He subtly implies that being showcased in the London gallery is payment enough, coupled with the vague promises of future income. By the way, there is no London gallery. Cedric probably gets paid by Hustletti, who moves the paintings on into Europe immediately. In short, he has become an absolute bastard ripping off young talent," rounded off Bobby.

"Have you an address for him?" fished Deborah.

"Still the same old Ma'am. Needing more," he said, with a teasing tone.

"Certainly," she said.

"Can you give me twenty-four hours please?"

"Between you and me Bobby," offered Deborah, "there is a container of art ready to go to Italy in two weeks, so twenty-four hours will be fine. Many thanks, Bobby. Isn't it time you retired?"

"Not while there are villains out there nicking irreplaceable art treasures. The garden can wait, so can the missus and her decorating list, refurbishing plans and cruises."

"Can't thank you enough," said Deborah.

"Just chip into my retirement present when I do decide to call it a day," suggested Bobby.

"Will do."

———

Twenty-four hours later an address was communicated to Deborah. It was in Cardiff.

"So, Cedric was probably covering Wales. I'm going to enjoy this," Deborah said to Yorrie, and chuckled.

"Me too."

"Just remember what Bernadette said – no heavy-handed methods," she reminded him.

"No, she said it to you, not me," chided Yorrie.

Deborah wagged her finger in his face. "You behave or I won't take you with me."

Yorrie shrugged. "Suit yourself, but remember, I know Cardiff like the back of my hand."

"Yes, the YMCA, the chip shops, and doss houses?" mocked Deborah playfully.

"And the Chinese takeaways!"

They both laughed, looking forward to the outing.

After breakfast the next day, followed by a relatively quick car journey, they arrived in Cardiff. Driving slowly along Port Road West, they passed a row of 1960s-built houses. Each one had a car in the drive and one out on the road, or tyre marks on the verge. Number 207 was no different.

Deborah pulled up on the opposite side of the road so they could watch and wait. The only information they had was Cedric's age and his address.

"Do you want something to eat? I'm starving," said Yorrie.

Deborah just nodded, not taking her eyes off the house, as Yorrie exited the car.

Whilst he was away, a weasel man of about sixty came out of the front door of number 207, with a handbag dog on a glittery lead. Cedric Perkins.

Deborah was out of her car like a shot. She locked the car, crossed over onto the same side as Cedric, and followed him, staying about forty yards behind. All the time she was looking out for Yorrie, but he was nowhere to be seen. Deborah groaned to herself. Here she was following a lead on an international art gang but where was her partner? Probably in a fish and chip shop queue waiting for haddock and chips twice with salt and extra vinegar. Maybe a pickled egg too.

Cedric headed towards a grassy area about four hundred yards along the road. As soon as he reached it, he unhitched the dog from its lead and told the dog to do a wee. Once it had performed, he instructed it to do a dump. It sniffed about on its way to a clump of grass and encouraged by an impatient master, dutifully performed. Cedric looked around to see if anyone was about and, when he locked eyes with Deborah, made a pretence of clearing it up. He then re-hitched the dog and started walking back to his way home.

When he was level with her, Deborah asked, "Cedric? Cedric Perkins? It is you, isn't it?"

He stopped. "Do I know you?"

"No, but I know you," said Deborah in her Chief Superintendent's voice. "Can we go somewhere to talk rather than in the road?"

"Look, I don't know who you are and I'm very busy, so if you will excuse me, I need to get back home."

Deborah crossed her arms and raised her chin. "You can either talk to me here or I will ring the police and you can have a conversation with them."

Cedric turned pale. "Who are you?"

"My name is Deborah Archer, and I am investigating a scam against artists in Wales."

Just then Yorrie joined them with his carrier bag of haddock and chips going colder by the second. Deborah introduced him.

"What do you want?" snapped Cedric at the pair of them.

"We want a list of all the artists you have duped into sending their paintings to a P.O. box number in London," said Deborah.

The old man tutted. "I haven't the foggiest idea what you are talking about, so if you'll excuse me, I need to get home."

As Cedric tugged the dog's lead and began to walk away,

Deborah pulled out her phone and dialled 999. She put it on speaker.

A voice asked, "Which service do you require?"

"Police, please," stated Deborah loudly.

Cedric turned back, scowling. "OK, OK, OK. Come back to the house and I'll talk to you."

Deborah ended the call. "Thank you," she said, very politely.

The three of them entered Cedric's house. It was clear to Deborah that it hadn't been decorated in fifty years. The hall walls were covered in thick, yellowing, anaglypta wallpaper, peeling from where it hadn't been stuck down properly. The carpets smelled of dog wee. The narrow runner up the stairs was threadbare and hazardous.

They followed Cedric into the back room and were instructed to sit down while he went to make some tea. The dog wouldn't leave Yorrie's bag of fish and chips alone, so he placed it on the table, and the dog promptly jumped onto a chair then up onto the table. This was obviously not the first time it had done this, and Deborah had visions of the dog eating off Cedric's plate whenever he left the room. The room smelled of old curtains, old furniture, old food, and old cigarette smoke.

A tussle began between the growling dog and Yorrie, and the bag split in the tug-o-war. Chips and fish spilled out all over the table and onto the floor. The dog immediately jumped down and started demolishing the food before Yorrie could stop it.

Deborah, noticing how thin the dog was, put her arm out to stop Yorrie from cleaning up. They stood back and watched the dog eat the food without it touching the sides. A piece of battered haddock disappeared in three bites and the scattered chips under the table were sought by smell and devoured. The dog then jumped back up onto a chair and then onto the table, but Yorrie was too quick and placed the remnants of the bag on the mantel piece. Desperate for the prize on the mantelpiece, the dog jumped off the table and proceeded to knock over the fireguard and compendium, making an almighty noise.

After a minute when Cedric hadn't come to investigate the noise, Deborah realised they had been so engrossed in the antics of the dog that they hadn't heard a sound from the kitchen. She flew out of the room and found the back door wide open.

Outside, the gate leading to the narrow back lane that ran between the back-to-back houses was also wide open. She shouted for Yorrie.

"You go out the back way and I'll go through the front door," she instructed. "Remember, Cedric's our only lead."

Yorrie ran down the garden path and out into the back lane.

Leaving the front door open, Deborah ran out into the road. Cedric was nowhere to be seen. She headed towards her car believing she could cover more ground that way. It fired up first time and with a squeal of rubber, she headed off westwards. After half a mile she knew Cedric could never have covered this distance and after a noisy U-turn, she headed back toward his house. She was cursing herself for allowing a dog to outwit them.

Deborah and Yorrie arrived at the corner of the road and the lane at exactly the same time, only to see Cedric coming out of a corner shop with a pint of milk.

Yorrie walked with him back to the house and a sheepish Deborah parked her car again and joined them inside.

"Boy, you two must be desperate to talk to me, tearing about Cardiff streets thinking I'd done a runner," said Cedric.

They re-entered the back room to find the dog fast asleep on the hearth rug. It had successfully reached the bag of fish and chips in their absence and finished them. Not a chip was left.

"OK, two things," snapped Cedric. "What do you want and what do I get for telling you?"

Yorrie threatened, "We want you to tell us the names and addresses of the artists you have duped, and for telling us their names and addresses, you get to avoid eating hospital food for about six weeks."

"So, let me get this straight," said Cedric. "If I tell you the artists' names, I avoid being hospitalised by you two, but I'd end up in hospital anyway thanks to the people I work for. And then, when I'm in the nick, I'd get the 'hot chocolate treatment' for being a grass and end up in hospital again. Doesn't seem like a good deal for me, does it?"

"What do you want then?" asked Deborah, knowing through experience that there were more ways to skin a cat than by ripping the fur off its back. Here was one slippery cat.

"I want a month's grace to get out of the country," he said.

Deborah shook her head. "We haven't got a month. We have seven days tops. We won't pass on your name to the police for seven days. Give us a dozen names, addresses and telephone numbers for us to verify here and now, and then you have seven clear days to go wherever you want."

Cedric considered the offer then added hesitantly, "And a grand."

"Piss off," snapped Deborah, losing patience.

"OK, OK." Cedric retrieved a small notebook from his sideboard. "Here's my address book of good artists who I really believe need better exposure." He handed it to Deborah.

She brought out her phone and rang the first number. No reply. She rang the second number and had the same result. She thumbed through the book and picked a name at random to ring. Third time lucky.

"Hallo, Poppy speaking."

Deborah put the phone on speaker before she spoke.

"Good afternoon, Poppy. I'm investigating a scam carried out on budding artists. Are you an artist?"

"I am, but who is this?"

"My name is Deborah, and my colleague and I are well on the way to breaking up this scam. Please will you help us? Have you sent any of your paintings to a P.O. box number in London on the promise of your art being displayed in a gallery in Chelsea?"

"Yes, stupidly I did. I sent three paintings and have been paid nothing at all. And if my husband catches the bastard who swindled me, he says he will swing for him."

Cedric went white.

"Well, your husband may not have that opportunity, but the gang who are causing the grief to young artists will soon be in prison."

After five more successful calls to irate artists, Deborah and Yorrie were convinced that there was enough evidence to go to the police.

"Right, that's my part of the bargain taken care of, so if you will kindly leave, I have some packing to do," said Cedric.

23

Susan was on a call from the agent dealing with the sale of her gallery. He began with an apology.

"There is a customer, but the customer was waiting for another deal to materialise before he could make an offer. He is now in a place where he can proceed. His has offered just below the asking price if you can exchange within six weeks."

Susan said, "Funny that. Right, undertake your due diligence on him and if he really is in a financial position to proceed, inform my solicitor. If he asks for any more money off or delays at all, withdraw the agreement immediately and put it back on the market. Is that clear?"

She hung up without waiting for a response to prepare for one of her estate agent viewings booked that week. After a race around her property with the vacuum cleaner and a check on the bathrooms, she was ready.

The agent arrived at the allotted time and Susan offered him coffee. After forty-five minutes, she was staggered to learn of the increase in the house's value. She commissioned the estate agent there and then and asked for a realistic time frame for a sale.

"Six weeks," he replied.

Her next trip was to Honest John's, which she arrived at just before closing. Both Giacomo and John were surprised to see her.

"What are you doing here?" asked Giacomo.

"Right, the three of us need to sit down now and have the conversation we planned to have in about six weeks. Things have changed and I want out!"

"Conversation? What conversation? Nobody told me about any conversation," said John.

Clearly fuming, Giacomo shot a look at Susan that said that her visit was going to be anything but amicable. She was heading for a confrontation with a capital C.

"Would one of you two tell me what the hell is going on?" demanded John.

He led the way into a back room and shouted for someone on the front desk to make some coffee and shut the betting shop for the night. He sat down and suggested the other two do the same.

Susan began, "I'm here because I want my share, and I want out!"

In came the coffee and John reinforced the request to shut up shop. "I don't give a toss what the time is. Shut the f***ing shop!"

Giacomo got up and started pacing. "Well, you're not getting anything till the next container – not the one in the yard but the container after that – has been shipped and the paintings have been sold. Got it?" he told Susan.

"Shush, let her finish," said John, motioning for Giacomo to return to his seat. "What's the reason you want out? Have you heard something?" John said quietly.

"No," said Susan.

"Then what the hell do you want?" Giacomo snarled, sitting back down.

"My personal circumstances have changed. Plus, I'm getting more and more uncomfortable about what we do, and my conscience won't let me do it anymore. So, I want out now."

"Bollocks!" shouted Giacomo. "You haven't got a conscience." He turned to John. "It's all because of this artist she has become infatuated with, called Drizzle. I told her not to get involved. Now she can't think straight." He tutted.

After some thought, John asked Susan, "What conversation were you going to have with me in six weeks' time that I know nothing about?"

"We – Giacomo and I – were going to give you the opportunity to run everything lock stock and barrel. We would have taken our share after the next container, and you could start running the whole show from then on. We wouldn't want anything from the business after that. Giacomo would go to Italy to live, and I would go to Antigua. After the split, we would never contact you or each other again. We cannot leave an audit trail. But I'm now getting stressed out about my part in all this, and I'm afraid I'll start making mistakes or raising suspicions. The risk of the scam being exposed is going up exponentially because of me."

"Yes," mumbled Giacomo.

"What about Cedric and Justin and all the other guys who are finders for us?" asked John.

"They would continue working for you. Doing the same thing. You take all the profit. You know all the contacts in Italy."

John stirred his coffee deliberately slowly, thinking. Susan hoped his avaricious side would surface.

"OK Giacomo, let's, just for the moment, assume we both agree to let Susan take her share and go. Susan leaving prevents further complications between the three of us or her making mistakes. Two of us means a bigger share. Her role in the scam is now minimal and her exiting won't hinder anything. If she goes, it will ensure there won't be any more conflict. And a smaller group attracts less scrutiny."

Giacomo thought for a while and finally muttered an agreement. "I just don't like changing the plan before the right time."

"OK then," said Susan with relief. "I take my current share now and when the next container is paid for, you send me my share of that. Then we part, never to communicate with each other again. Deal?"

John nodded. "It's a deal."

Giacomo also said, "It's a deal." But followed it up with something unpleasant in Italian.

"Then that's settled," said Susan. "Giacomo, I suggest you collect your things at the earliest time as I am putting the house on the market and will need to show people around."

Giacomo grunted in response. John offered for him to stay at his flat as it was only for a short time.

"Oh, and one last thing, I want Dazzle's last painting back. The one you brought in this morning," said Susan.

"No chance." Giacomo walked over to the table where the painting had been placed, ready to be repacked.

John joined him and said, "I was really impressed with this one. In fact, I would have bought it myself." With that, he took the painting from Giacomo, opened the packaging fully and held it up to the light.

Susan jumped up and tried to grab the painting, knocking Giacomo in the process. He stumbled into John, who nearly dropped the painting, and in the melee, the frame became slightly distorted and out fell the tracker. The three of them watched as it bounced noisily on the floor, spun around and around, and finally settled on one side.

Giacomo picked it up. "It's a f***ing tracker! Is this why you wanted out, you bitch? Is this why you wanted the painting so badly, 'cos you knew it was bugged?" he shouted menacingly at Susan.

"You stupid oaf!" she snapped at him. "If I had known about it, I could have taken it out last night, couldn't I? The question is what the hell are we going to do with it now?"

John was ashen but quickly took control. "Get that container out of my yard tonight. It doesn't matter that it isn't full. It needs to be on a ferry first thing in the morning."

Giacomo nodded and started making calls to drivers.

"What about the tracker?" asked Susan.

"I'll put it on a painting of a similar size to that one then get it on a lorry going north tonight," said John, taking his phone out of his pocket to make a call. "Whoever is following it will be on a wild goose chase till dawn. That will give us a little more time to tidy things up. By tomorrow, my office and yard will be all cleaned up with no trace of any paintings whatsoever, so we should be in the clear."

There was quiet in the room while each digested the seriousness of the situation. John broke the silence. "Tomorrow, Susan you split the money three ways. Get our shares to us by first thing, and I mean first thing! You take yours and disappear. We can all breathe easily then."

Susan said, "Give me the painting and I'll get rid of it tomorrow. And just for the record, you two, I really didn't know anything about the tracker."

24

Deborah and Yorrie were on their third coffee waiting for the call from A. B. Chevron. The phone hadn't ring twice before she was up, had taken two paces across the room, and answered it.

Yorrie was immediately by her side.

"Hello, Bernadette. What's your news?" asked Deborah.

"Some good, some bad," replied Bernadette. "Apparently, the container left Honest Johns at 4.00 a.m. this morning on its way to Southampton. This was not the plan. The container was originally booked on a ferry in about two weeks' time, as I told you, but the tracker and painting are now being delivered somewhere else. A UK police surveillance vehicle followed it to a service station on the M1, and then it headed north. They have narrowed it down to a lorry with the company name of *North East Roofers* who are based in Durham. So, the UK police are following the tracker and painting and have passed the container details on to Interpol, who will follow it all the way to Italy."

"OK. Anything else?"

"Yes, we have some news on Justin Caldwell, the finder we were following," said Bernadette. "He was not very forthcoming at first. My agent spoke with him in a pub where he swore blind that he knew nothing about any scam aimed at artists. My agent was at a loss about what to do. However, as luck would have it, one of the aggrieved artists spotted him in the pub and had a massive row with him there and then. There's no temper like a woman scorned or stolen from. She called him everything from a pig to a dog. My agent quietened her, despite all the tears, and asked her to sit down with them to sort it all out. Justin listened and said he would make it all up to her. He even handed her £300 in cash as a start. She eventually left, after leaving all her contact details with my agent."

"That sounds positive," said Deborah.

"Indeed. Justin then furtively suggested to my agent that maybe there was a compromise that could be agreed between just the two of them 'man to man'. If my agent gave him five days to leave the country, he would give him the names of all the artists he had scammed. My agent let him hang himself – listening to his confession before uncovering a tape of the conversation. After Justin gave him the list of names, my agent rang two of the artists at random to make sure they were legit. Convinced they were, he contacted the police and handed everything over, including Justin Perkins. How about you. How did you get on with Cedric?" asked Bernadette.

"He was quite forthcoming eventually and gave us his address book. We rang a few scammed victims too. One of them – a young artist by the name of Poppy – has a husband who promised to kill Cedric, so the rest was easy."

"Great, where is he now?"

"Unfortunately, he did a runner, and we lost him," replied Deborah, straight-faced.

Yorrie was listening in and his eyes went up into his head at the size of the lie.

"Never mind," said Bernadette. "At least now the police have Justin, and we have the address book from Cedric, which we will pass on to them."

"What's next then?" asked Deborah.

"The police are planning a swoop tomorrow to arrest Susan Cartwright, Giacomo Hustletti and Honest John, and I wondered if you two would like to be in at the kill, as it were?"

"Can we invite Dazzle?" whispered Yorrie. Deborah relayed his question.

"I don't see why not. Meet me three streets to the west of Honest John's at 5.00 a.m. tomorrow morning."

"Will do. See you tomorrow, Bernadette."

"Wow," said Yorrie excitedly. "I can't believe we'll all be in at the kill!"

"Don't look forward to it too much yet. Remember, if Dazzle is going to be there, we need to tell him the whole story first," said Deborah.

"Hmm," replied Yorrie, more subdued now. "I must admit, that's not a thought I'm relishing, especially as it includes the serious possibility of me becoming homeless."

———

Yorrie told Dazzle that Deborah had invited him to join them for an early dinner. Vegetable casserole had long since lost its appeal, so Dazzle welcomed the chance to eat meat in the company of friends.

A bottle of wine was already on the table, and he was offered a beer as soon as he arrived at Deborah's house. They all settled down and began to talk light heartedly.

At the end of the first course Deborah announced, "Dazzle, we have something to tell you."

Immediately, he assumed they were to get engaged, but their expressions became apprehensive.

"What is it?" he asked.

"We know where your paintings are – they're in Italy!" Yorrie blurted out.

"Italy? Why – has someone bought them?" Dazzle asked, and sipped his wine.

"No, they've all been stolen from you," announced Yorrie.

Dazzle's eyes opened wide, and he swallowed his wine with difficulty.

Deborah took over, the balm to Yorrie's abruptness. "What I'm going to tell you may hurt, but it will explain a few things. It will also make you angry and will stretch our friendship to breaking point."

Dazzle looked quizzically at her.

"Yorrie and I could not stand by for a moment longer and watch you being fleeced, so we set out on a journey to find your paintings. In so doing, we discovered some unpleasant facts about a very big scam against UK artists that has been going on for a couple of years. You have been caught up in it. What happened to you with Susan is being replicated all around the country. A number of finders seduce artists into sending their paintings to be displayed in a London gallery by promising them more and more money. I'm sorry, Dazzle, but there is no gallery in London."

"No, no," said Dazzle, shaking his head. "I can't believe that Susan is caught up in anything like that. We have a very special relationship that goes back donkey's years. She is very close to me. I trust her. You must have made a mistake."

Deborah sighed softly. "Dazzle, there is no simple way to tell you this. I do believe you and Susan had a special relationship that under any other circumstances could have become permanent. However, she is one of two people who run the whole UK operation."

She stopped for Yorrie to pour them all more wine. He couldn't make eye contact with Dazzle.

"Why didn't you tell me all this weeks ago?" asked Dazzle.

"Because this has come to a head in the last week," Deborah told him. "We engaged a relatively new company called A. B. Chevron, which is based in London and run by Bernadette Westerman, the MD. It was recommended to me by some old, well-respected police colleagues who work in the art recovery business. A. B. Chevron quickly discovered that what had happened to you was happening in various parts of the country at the same time." She gave him a sympathetic smile.

"The only tiny piece of good news is that the finders for the scam are professionals and only select paintings of very high quality. All the paintings are then posted to London and when they have a container load, it is shipped to Italy where there is a much higher demand for good watercolours. None of the artists are paid, except occasionally for the first painting. So, Bernadette suggested we hide a tracker in one of your paintings and send it as normal."

Dazzle looked at Yorrie, who blushed and looked away.

"When your painting reached London," Deborah continued, "the tracker signal was received and followed, at a distance, by agents of A. B. Chevron. They then passed it over to the police who have been following it ever since." She stopped to take another drink and to let Dazzle process the news.

Dazzle just shook his head again, unable to comprehend what had just been relayed to him.

"At the moment, your painting, along with the tracker, is on its way up north. We don't know why or where yet. And a container full of paintings is queueing for a ferry at Southampton docks, ready to travel to Italy when the weather improves. Interpol are going to follow it to its destination and hopefully round up the whole scam operation in Europe. Tomorrow morning the police are going to swoop and arrest the three main UK scammers, including Susan. You can be there, if you want, to see the winding up of this dreadful affair. We thought it might offer you some closure. We will be leaving here at 3.00 a.m. sharp."

Yorrie winced at the mention of the early start.

"Yorrie and I have to go to give statements to the police. We would completely understand if you felt it would be too awful for you to be present," Deborah said, patting Dazzle's arm.

Dazzle thought for a long time, then drained his wine. "Thank you for a lovely meal, Deborah, but I will not be joining you tomorrow." Without saying another word, he nodded goodnight and left.

Yorrie and Deborah shook their tired heads, mutually agreeing that it had been a perfectly natural reaction from someone who does not do confrontation.

"Right," said Yorrie. "We've got an early start. Let's call it a night."

25

Deborah put the key in the ignition at 2.59 a.m. precisely. Yorrie clicked his seat belt beside her one minute later. Nothing was stirring in the quiet seaside town street.

"Let's go to London then," she said, and flicked the headlights on, which immediately silhouetted a man standing close by. He was standing under a tree in a thick, dark jacket and his hood was up against the sea fret. Her windscreen wipers squeaked, blurring the windscreen as they tried to clear the salty sea-fret. The man started to walk unhurriedly towards the car.

Unnerved, Deborah remembered one of her colleagues, Bobby, saying, 'Beware, Ma'am, these villains are not people to be trifled with. The rewards are immense, and they'll have you killed if you jeopardise their income. Nothing stops these people.' She gunned the car out into the empty road.

The man quickly walked out in front of the car and raised his arm. Did he have a gun? Not waiting to find out the hard way if the man was about to fire two shots through the window, she turned the steering wheel abruptly and narrowly missed him. Yorrie turned to look and suddenly shouted for Deborah to stop.

"It's Dazzle!"

Dazzle approached the car and Deborah wound down her window. "I reflected on what you two said last night and decided I was being churlish," he said. "You have both put a huge amount of work into helping me. I need to put the whole sordid business to bed once and for all. Please may I come too?"

"Of course, we're pleased to have you with us," said Yorrie. "None of it felt quite right without you."

Dazzle piled into the back seat of the little car and asked for a repeat blow-by-blow discussion on their activities.

"I just want to get the scam and the current police investigation all clear in my head," he explained.

Two hours later, they pulled into a cul-de-sac amongst a dozen police cars. Deborah parked then went to find Bernadette and her contact in the police. She soon came back and explained the plan.

"Apparently, we are to remain here until the police raid has been completed and the villains have been apprehended. Then we can go inside the premises and be briefed on the situation by the Superintendent. Then all three of us will be asked to give statements. Are you two OK with that?"

"Is Susan here?" asked Dazzle.

"No idea, but one of the constables said she left her house early this morning in her car. The police are mounting the raid in five minutes. This is the bit I love; after all the tedious work there's a collar. You two stay here, and someone will come for you when it's all safe."

"Where are you going?" asked Yorrie.

"I wouldn't miss this for all the world," said Deborah, and smiled. Then she was gone.

————

"What are we going to do?" asked Yorrie

"I'm definitely staying here," said Dazzle. "I don't want to see Susan put in handcuffs. I still have some feelings for her."

"OK, but I'm going to keep an eye on Deborah and make sure she's safe. Mind you, anyone who has a nickname of 'Fang' probably doesn't need nobody to make sure she's safe."

With that, he slipped out of the car. He noted that all the police on foot were headed at a trot for the betting shop, and so followed them.

The police cars had already moved closer to the shop front and the yard entrance.

————

Deborah followed the police as they burst into the betting shop. Giacomo and John were calmly sitting in the office drinking tea when all hell broke loose. Police in riot gear were everywhere, shouting for everyone to get down. The teller at the grill screamed. But Giacomo and John just sat there.

John asked, "How can I help you then, officers?"

The police stopped shouting at the quiet pair, clearly not expecting to have had the wind taken out of their sails.

Deborah's professional eye was everywhere, but there was nothing to find. The place was clean. Overly clean.

The yard was inspected, the toilets were inspected, the roof was inspected, and the office was inspected, but nothing incriminating was found. John's accounts were in a folder on his desk, ready for inspection.

"Where's Susan?" asked Deborah. Bernadette stood close behind her.

"Susan who?" asked Giacomo.

"Susan Cartwright. The woman you live with."

Giacomo shrugged. "I rent a room from Susan. I do not live with her, as you say."

"Whatever. Where is she?" asked Bernadette.

"No idea."

Yorrie, who had entered the office minutes earlier, suggested he would let Dazzle know Susan wasn't around.

————

Back at the car, Dazzle's face was expressionless.

"OK, I'll stay here or have a walk while you give your statements at the police station. I'll see you there later."

Yorrie nodded and returned to the betting shop.

Dazzle hailed a black cab and told the driver where to go. A hunch from an alcohol-fuelled conversation he and Susan had enjoyed late one night led him to pull up outside The Clover Hotel. It was her favourite hotel in all of London. She had said that if she was to ever leave the UK, she would want The Clover Hotel in London to be her lasting memory. He knew by now she could be on a plane to who knew where, and that this was a very long shot, but hey-ho.

He paid the driver and walked into the opulent foyer. In front of the acre of reception desk, he asked if a Miss Susan Cartwright had checked in.

"Yes, sir. She's in the cocktail lounge having a coffee. You've only just caught her for she has ordered a taxi in a few minutes," answered the helpful receptionist.

Dazzle made his way to the cocktail bar and looked about. In a corner, Susan was watching the world go by through the floor-to-ceiling Victorian windows. She had her back to the door. He approached her, shouldering a mix of hurt and determination.

"May I buy the lady a drink?" he asked.

As soon as she heard his voice, she spun around and faced him. Her startled expression turned into a coy smile.

"I didn't expect to see you here," she exclaimed.

"Clearly, but neither did I expect to see you running off with a piece of my soul. I assume that's one of mine." He nodded towards the package leaning against her chair.

Glancing at the package then briefly back at him, she commented, "It's your best work yet. I just couldn't leave without it. You should be flattered."

Dazzle took a seat opposite her and leaned forward. "I'm not flattered at all, Susan. I'm hurt, really hurt. I trusted you absolutely. I look back and wonder if any of our time together was real?"

Looking defensive but clearly trying to remain composed, she said, "Of course it was real, but you will never understand why I did this. It's not a betrayal; its plain and simple survival."

"Try me. I've all the time in the world."

Dazzle sat back, waiting for a lengthy explanation.

She looked at her watch and settled back in her chair too.

"It should never have happened; you and me, that is. That was never part of the methodology of the scam. We set out to collect top of the range watercolour paintings from around the UK and sell them into Europe, then you bounced into my world and upset everything, tumbling me, my head and my heart. I had a wonderful time with you, Dazzle, and I'm staggered at how good you've become as an artist. Much better than I will ever be. But I was in the scam too deep and couldn't extricate myself. I was funding some pretty evil people who I was, and still am, very frightened of." Susan sighed. "I can keep saying sorry till the cows come home, but it won't make any difference now. It's all too late."

There was real regret in her tone.

Dazzle didn't say a word, and just listened. After a long silence he said, "You do know that Giacomo and Honest John have been arrested and are now in the police station following their arrest, giving statements. Don't you? You do know that Interpol are following the container of paintings and will clean up the Italian side of the business. Don't you? You do know that Justin is in custody in the north and

Cedric is on the run somewhere in Wales. Don't you? It will only be a matter of time until they find you."

This was clearly all a shock to Susan, as it showed.

"I think you have about twenty-four hours of freedom left then it will be your turn." His tone was emotionless.

Tears filled Susan's eyes. "No, no, I can't go to prison. Will you help me please, Dazzle?"

"No!" said Dazzle, angry at being asked after everything she had done.

"You can have your painting back. I only wanted to take it with me because it kept me close to you."

Dazzle looked away. This was a very different woman from who he had first seen confidently sipping her coffee on her way to a new life.

"Here." Susan handed over the painting to Dazzle, who ripped open the packaging to confirm it was his original. Satisfied he asked," What help do you want?"

"Forty-eight hours before you go to the police."

"What do I get for giving you that?"

"I'll tell you where two more of your paintings are."

Dazzle thought for a moment and said, "OK."

"I sent two of your paintings to two different art valuation houses and paid for the service in advance. Your first painting is with a valuation house who are masters in the art of understatement, so don't be too upset by their valuations. They suggested that, if your first painting of St. Cuthbert's Bay cliff was displayed in a gallery where the proprietor had a good sense of light to show it off to its best advantage, it could probably fetch £2,000. If it went to a UK auction, it could fetch £2,500. If it went on an international auction, it could fetch £3,000," said Susan.

Dazzle nodded and gestured for her to go on.

"Your other painting is the one of the tide re-entering the rock pools where the sea weed appears to be moving. It's with a more ambitious valuation house. They believe it would double all of the estimates from the other company. I'll contact both valuation houses and tell them you will be coming in personally to collect the paintings. Don't forget your I.D. And, of course, I'll pay you what I owe you. So, is it a deal?" she asked.

"Yes, it's a deal. I'll keep quiet for forty-eight hours."

The Clover Hotel receptionist came into the bar to inform them that a taxi had arrived for Miss Cartwright.

Susan kissed Dazzle on the cheek and left. He didn't get up but watched her go. With her seemed to go all his imagined longing. With her went the huge weight that was holding him in the past. He felt lighter. His future was now clear.

————

"Where to, miss?' the taxi driver asked Susan.

"Just drive," she told him.

When far enough away from the hotel she asked to be driven to a taxi rank, where she got in the front taxi. She asked that driver to circle the block to make sure she hadn't been followed, then met up again with the first taxi driver for her journey to East Midlands Airport. She agreed to pay three quarters of the fare up front. Having just heard from

Dazzle that Giacomo and Honest John were in a police station, she was taking no chances.

When well away from London, Susan instructed the driver to take her to a post office. There, she sent a money order to Dazzle's home address for twice what she owed him. She felt better.

In East Midlands Airport departure area, she moved between coffee bars, constantly on the lookout. Shortly after, she exited the airport and took a bus to Nottingham, where she boarded a train to York.

Half an hour later, comfortably seated in the first-class carriage with a drink and some nibbles, she watched the lights of the countryside speed by as she left the south and her fears further and further behind her. It had been an exhausting day, but she felt pleased with herself. Smiling, she gently stroked her tummy with both hands and whispered, "I just hope you are half as good an artist as your daddy!"

26

Dazzle arrived back at Deborah's car later that morning, having posted his painting back to his home address. Deborah explained to him that Yorrie was still giving his statement. With a smile, she explained that, being Welsh, he was making the most of his five minutes of fame and War and Peace was probably being re-written, embellished and improved. Dazzle understood exactly what she meant and smiled too

Deborah turned, looking for someone. "I want to introduce you to Bernadette Westerman, the MD of A. B. Chevron. Ah, here she–"

She didn't finish her sentence before Dazzle exclaimed, "Mandy!" He walked over and kissed her. She kissed him back and hugged him, the type of hug someone gives when they don't want to let go. He kissed her again.

Just then Yorrie arrived at the car and echoed, "Mandy! Good grief, what the hell are you doing here?"

"Hello Yorrie." Mandy was delighted to see him and also gave him a hug. "I'm so pleased to see you both."

Deborah put her hand up and said, "Mandy? Bring me up to speed please, someone? Anyone?"

Bernadette jumped in. "Deborah, my full name is Amanda Bernadette Westerman. I met Dazzle when Yorrie sold me a BOGOF painting that he shouldn't have on St. Cuthbert's Bay promenade nearly three years ago. Then, when my husband came looking for me at Dazzle's house, Yorrie punched him, causing a cut to his head that needed five stitches, broke two of his ribs, split his lip and broke his nose!"

Bernadette, a.k.a. Mandy, smiled and rubbed Yorrie's arm. "Incidentally, that day was also the last day of our marriage." Deborah shook her bewildered head. "It was Dazzle who helped me clarify all my thoughts about my future in one wonderful dinner, followed by a week in St. Cuthbert's Bay that I will never forget," said Mandy, looking at Dazzle affectionately.

She recounted the consequences of their meeting, "A. B. Chevron, my detective agency, is the result of that week and I started using my second name Bernadette as I thought it sounded more professional. I can't thank him enough." Mandy looked into Dazzle's eyes and smiled as she explained the effect he'd had on her.

"Am I missing something?" asked Deborah.

Bernadette continued, "My company had been working with the police on a big art theft, and we'd had a stroke of good luck by pulling off the biggest success of A. B. Chevron's short life. By sheer chance, Deborah, you rang and asked for my help. I think you knew someone in the police who had worked on the same big art theft.

"That would have been Snoz," interjected Yorrie.

"Snoz?" asked Dazzle.

"Don't ask," said Yorrie.

Mandy shook her head. "I had no idea that the person you were representing was Dazzle."

Deborah said, "I need a drink. A bloody big one!"

"To the pub it is then!" said Yorrie.

Dazzle, still staggered by the valuation of his paintings, the successful launch of the gallery in his home town, and was now completely rid of the ghost of Susan. Now he was walking on air towards a pub, arm in arm with Mandy, the owner of her own up-and-coming detective agency. Life finally felt amazing for him.

To Dazzle's surprise, fifty Yards from the pub, Yorrie stopped dead in his tracks, and dropped onto one knee. Deborah gasped in shock.

"Deborah Archer, would you do me the great honour of marrying me?"

Smiling, she said, "Thank the Lord for that. I thought you would never ask. Of course I'll marry you. I can't think of anyone in the world more crackers with whom I would like to spend the rest of my life." She pulled him up and kissed him lovingly.

Dazzle and Mandy clapped and cheered.

"Is there a ring?" Deborah asked tentatively after the kiss. "Just thought I'd ask."

"Oh, I haven't bought it yet, have I? You know, just in case!"

Deborah rolled her eyes affectionately and everyone laughed.

ACKNOWLEDGEMENTS

My special thanks go to my editor-in-chief Claire Jennison, of C. L. Jennison Editorial, for her patience, help and sensitive guidance.

OTHER BOOKS BY
HOWARD G AWBERY

Five Strange Tales

The Music Box

Me and My Lamp

The Odd Noble Deed

Isobelle

Five Even Stranger Tales

Five Coffee Time Tales

A Sprig of Mint

Don't Eat the Sandwiches!

Bethesda

Crumpets

FIVE STRANGE TALES

A cat with attitude, green-fingered garden gnomes, a Roman helmet, and two fiercely protective ghosts feature in this delightful anthology.

Each one of the *Five Strange Tales* has been written to accompany a cup of tea and a biscuit, whilst pleasantly disorientating the reader and challenging what they believe to be 'real' for a few moments.

When finished, the book will be lovingly replaced on the coffee table, leaving the reader smiling to themselves and wondering could that actually happen?

THE MUSIC BOX

In 1938, with preparations for war well under way, newlyweds Celia and Carsten Prestwick begin their honeymoon on the night train to Scotland.

Sabotage, a steam train race, and two tangled love triangles are just some of the issues that tumble out of this intriguing romantic novel; a novel peppered with classic Howard G. Awbery twists and turns.

Readers will be able to put *The Music Box* down just once...at the very end!

ME AND MY LAMP

Dr Howard G. Awbery joined the British coal mining industry as a fresh faced eighteen-year-old and emerged thirty years later, battered and bruised but worldlier for the richness of the experience.

In this captivating book, *Me and My Lamp*, he recounts stories from those years. Stories of human kindness, national coal strikes, personal injury, a ghostly warning, and the eclectic family of miners who made him laugh, and cry.

As one of the few colliers left who once filled a 'stint' of coal using a shovel and set wooden props to secure the roof, he draws the reader into an underground world that those who have never ventured shudder to imagine. However, his world of coal was not a black world at all, for his mining stories depict a bright, colourful world, full of excitement, challenge, and amazing people.

THE ODD NOBLE DEED

The Rangemore Hotel is a tired, Victorian hotel struggling to survive on the North Wales coastline. A coastline owned by the sea, loaned by the sea, and at any time, could be reclaimed by the sea.

Equally as unpredictable as the sea are the fortunes of the owners and staff of The Rangemore Hotel, the backdrop to *The Odd Noble Deed*.

Four people associated with this once grand hotel tumble and crash into each other's lives. Passion, treachery and lies leave only two winners.

Or are they winners? For to win, one must truly value the prize.

ISOBELLE

Never in a million years could Isobelle have imagined that any one customer would make so much difference to her life. One day, however, into her busy London boutique came such a customer. 'Shoulders' as she derogatorily referred to him, rocked her equilibrium and tumbled her settled, solitary, secure life over and over again.

Before 'Shoulders', Isobelle's independence was her armour against all-comers; she believed her life and emotions impenetrable. As she reluctantly became increasingly embroiled in this customer's complex life, she realised how wrong she was.

FIVE EVEN STRANGER TALES

Howard G. Awbery has done it again. An intriguing follow-on from *Five Strange Tales*, *Five Even Stranger Tales* will not disappoint.

With your log burner blazing and a steaming cup of frothy, hot chocolate by your side, these creative and carefully crafted tales will keep you guessing until the final line.

Mix seagulls and weddings with philanthropy and a doctor's computer with a mind of its own, and you won't have any idea what's coming next.

Cantering through an eclectic gathering of characters, you will finally come to rest on an allotment in the company of a tramp called Humphrey. But all is not as it appears...

FIVE COFFEE TIME TALES

Definition: Special moments, planned for and dedicated to drinking coffee. Coffee time is instead of work, not with work, culminating in an 'ahrrrr' sound.

Planning for coffee time: Mobiles out of reach, frustrating Sudoku out of sight, to-do lists away, and who cares if imbroglio is a real word in today's crossword?

Adding joy: Only one thing can improve coffee time – a good book. Howard G. Awbery's *Five Coffee Time Tales* includes charming short stories, each with a 'Well, I really didn't expect that!' twist, to be read in the time it takes to drink a cup of coffee.

Enjoy your coffee.

A SPRIG OF MINT

An interest in ancient stone circles keeps James, a financial trader in the city of London, well-grounded. When visiting a little-known stone circle in North Wales, on the summer solstice, he is transported back to the time of the circle's construction. James lives among the Late Bronze Age villagers, befriending the architect of the stone circle, Barnaby, and a young widow, Eira.

James rejoins the present, quickly realising he was far happier in the past than his current, shallow London life. He returns to the past only to find it under siege by the Hunllef, a warring, wandering tribe. Following a bloody battle he and Eira escape to the present.

Beth, a PhD student studying the history of stone circles, befriends James and Eira and becomes entangled in their lives spanning two time zones.

DON'T EAT THE SANDWICHES!

Don't Eat the Sandwiches! is a story set in 1975, of two cousins in their mid-thirties whose lives bounce back together.

Despite Joanne, an accountant by profession, vowing never, ever to go on holiday again with "Let's drink Malaga dry!" Veronica, she hears the announcement, "Ladies and gentlemen, please fasten your seat belts, we will shortly be landing at Costa del Sol airport."

Returning from their holiday peeling and poor, they hatch a late night gin and paella-fuelled plan. Sending Veronica to work in a care home seems the obvious source of new guests for Joanne's newly acquired, failing, funeral parlour.

However, providence has other ideas in this tale of comeuppance woven by Howard G. Awbery.

BETHESDA

BETHESDA
A sequel to 'Don't Eat the Sandwiches'

Howard G Awbery

Bethesda Residential Home for the Active Elderly is well on her way to becoming the UK South Coast's Residential Home of First Choice, all thanks to her formidable managing director, Veronica Puxworthy.

For the past four years, since unexpectedly inheriting Bethesda in 1975, Veronica and her motley crew of managers have worked hard to make it a success. But now, after a series of surprise attacks, that success is under serious threat.

Can Veronica and her team – her cousin Joanne, an ex-convict and ex-accountant; Vincent, an ex-hearse driver with useful mates in the underworld; Elsie, Vincent's wife, a medium and ex-embalmer; Alejandro, a hot-tempered Spaniard and head chef; Rosie, Alejandro's naïve but sweet wife; and, finally, Godfrey, the quintessentially English, pipe-smoking, meticulous groundsman – overcome the unscrupulous attackers?

With a little help from an extraordinary source, they devise a plan to protect their beloved Bethesda. Can they save her from further attacks before it's too late?

CRUMPETS

Broken hearted as well as broke, Emma invests everything she has left into a decaying, derelict ex-funeral parlour on dingy, run-down Bucket Street. Her rose-tinted vision and unwavering enthusiasm help bring the soul of the building back to life.

But it's not the only soul she discovers as age-old secrets soon surface...

However, as *Crumpets* café begins to thrive, and Emma's hard work begins to pay off, her dream quickly becomes a nightmare. Local protection racketeers, underhand property company dealings and secret council plans for a bypass threaten Emma's newly built business.

Can the unlikely friends she has made along the way help her protect *Crumpets* and its wonderful, close-knit community?

Printed in Dunstable, United Kingdom